THE RUBADUB MYSTERY

This Armada book belongs to:

_____

_____

_____

Other titles by Enid Blyton in Armada

Brownie Tales
A Book of Fairies
Mr. Galliano's Circus
Hurrah for the Circus!
Circus Days Again
Come to the Circus
The Naughtiest Girl in the School
The Naughtiest Girl Again
The Naughtiest Girl is a Monitor
The Adventurous Four
The Adventurous Four Again
The Ragamuffin Mystery
The Rockingdown Mystery
The Ring O'Bells Mystery
The Rilloby Fair Mystery
The Rat-a-tat Mystery
The Secret of Killimooin
The Secret Mountain
The Secret of Spiggy Holes
The Secret of Moon Castle
Happy Day Stories
Rainy Day Stories
The Six Bad Boys
The Put-Em-Rights
The Children at Green Meadows
The Children of Willow Farm
Adventures on Willow Farm
Six Cousins at Mistletoe Farm
The Children of Cherry Tree Farm
Six Cousins Again
Those Dreadful Children
Holiday House
Picnic Party
Storytime Book
The Family at Red-Roofs

THE RUBADUB MYSTERY

Enid Blyton

First published in the U.K. in 1951 by
William Collins Sons & Co. Ltd., London and Glasgow.
This edition was first published in 1969 by
William Collins Sons & Co. Ltd., 14 St. James's Place,
London SW1A 1PF

© Enid Blyton 1951

Printed in Great Britain by
Love & Malcomson Ltd.,
Brighton Road, Redhill, Surrey.

CONDITIONS OF SALE:
This book is sold subject to the condition
that it shall not, by way of trade or otherwise,
be lent, re-sold, hired out or otherwise circulated
without the publisher's prior consent in any form of
binding or cover other than that in which it is
published and without a similar condition
including this condition being imposed
on the subsequent purchaser.

CHAPTER ONE

PLANS FOR A HOLIDAY

"Snubby!" called a cross voice. "SNUBBY! Didn't I tell you to tie Loony up?"

Snubby came flying downstairs to his aunt. "Oh, Aunt Susan, I did! Has he got loose again? Oh, I say—did he make all that mess in the hall?"

The black spaniel sat in the middle of a few sheets of torn-up newspaper, his tongue hanging out. He looked exactly as if he was grinning.

"That's your uncle's morning newspaper," said his aunt. "He hasn't even read it yet. Snubby, you know that we're very rushed trying to get everything done before we leave to-day. I really *can* not have Loony rushing about loose."

"I'll shut Loony into my room, Mother," said Diana,

coming up. "And I'll lock the door and put the key in my pocket. Then Loony will be safe."

"Well, nothing else in your room will be safe!" said Mrs. Lynton. "Do what you like with him—but keep him out of my way this morning! We shall never get off this afternoon, your father and I."

The Lyntons were going to America for a few weeks. The three children and Loony the dog were going off to the sea with Miss Pepper, Mrs. Lynton's old governess. She often had charge of them when the Lyntons had to go away.

Snubby had only arrived the day before, having spent the first week of the holidays with some other cousins. He had no parents and spent his time staying with various relations—but of them all he much preferred the Lyntons. He was very fond of his Aunt Susan, and admired and respected his Uncle Richard. His uncle, however, neither admired nor respected Snubby.

"I consider that boy to be the world's worst nuisance," was his continual description of poor Snubby.

Loony was led upstairs by a firm Diana. Sardine the cat was waiting for him at a turn of the stairs and leapt at him. He sprang back, almost pulling Diana down the stairs, and she squealed.

"This house is a mad-house," said her father, at the top of the stairs. "Where's Miss Pepper? Can't she take you all into some quiet corner till we've gone? America will seem a place of utter peace and quiet after this. Really, when you children come back from school, it's . . ."

"Oh, Daddy—you always say that," said Diana, hauling Loony up by his lead. "You know you'll miss us when you go. Daddy, I wish you'd take us with you to America."

"Not on your life!" said her father, horrified. "You'd probably all fall overboard, to start with—and Snubby would spend his time down in the engine-room with Roger . . ."

"Oh, I say, sir—should I be allowed to?" called Snubby. "That would be smashing."

"Where do you get those awful words from?" said his uncle. "Can't you talk Queen's English?"

"I bet the Queen says 'smashing' sometimes," argued Snubby. "I bet she . . ."

"Move aside and let me pass," said his uncle impatiently. "What with Diana and the dog on the stairs, and now you—and is that Sardine I see waiting for me to fall over her as usual—this is a real mad-house."

"Richard dear—do come down and help me with the labelling," called Mrs. Lynton. "We'll go into the study and shut the door and the windows, and see if we can't keep out all the riff-raff!"

"Gosh—fancy Aunt Susan calling us riff-raff," said Snubby indignantly. "Hey, Aunt Susan . . ."

A door slammed down below. Snubby gave it up. He helped to push the reluctant Loony along the landing to Diana's bedroom.

Miss Pepper was there, pulling clothes out of drawers and cupboards. The children were to go to the seaside the next day, and Miss Pepper was trying to do a little sorting and packing in between helping Mrs. Lynton.

"Hallo, Miss Pepper," said Snubby, as if he hadn't seen her for a month. He gave her a sudden squeeze round the waist. She gasped.

"*Don't*, Snubby! Why so affectionate all of a sudden? What is it you want out of me now?"

"Nothing," said Snubby, looking hurt. "I just felt sort of thrilled—holidays, you know—no more work for ages —going off to the sea to-morrow. What's the place we're going to, Miss Pepper? Nobody's told me anything yet."

Roger came marching in, his arms full of swim-suits. "Here you are, Miss Pepper," he said, putting them down on the bed. "I've found three swim-suits each. Is that enough?"

"Good gracious yes," said Miss Pepper. "Oh, don't let Loony get hold of them. Snubby, take him away."

"He's supposed to be locked up here in Diana's bedroom," said Snubby.

"Well, he can't be," said Miss Pepper decidedly. "I'm doing a lot of sorting out in here and I don't intend to be locked in with Loony or any other mad dog either."

"He's not mad," said Snubby. "Are you, Loony?"

Loony promptly lay down on his back and pedalled his feet in the air, looking sideways for Snubby's admiring remarks.

"Bicycle away," said Miss Pepper to Loony. "Stay there

on your back and pedal for the rest of the morning. That will suit me nicely."

"Nobody's told me *yet* where we're going to-morrow," said Snubby plaintively.

"Well, you only came yesterday," said Roger. "And considering that you spent practically the whole evening describing the cricket match you played in last Saturday, and told us about every run you didn't get, and how many sweaters the umpire wore, and what you'd do if *you* were chosen for the Test team, and . . ."

"That's not funny," said Snubby. "Miss Pepper do tell me about to-morrow."

"Well, we start off early, and we catch the train to Woodlingham, and we change there, and we catch another train, a slow one, to Rockypool, and then we get a taxi to Rubadub," said Miss Pepper. "There—now you know, so stop asking me."

"Rubadub! I don't believe it! There's not a place called Rubadub!" exclaimed Snubby disbelievingly.

"There is," said Diana. "It's marked on the map. I think it's a super name. I love thinking I'm going to stay at Rubadub. Miss Pepper used to stay there when she was small—didn't you, Miss Pepper?"

"Yes," said Miss Pepper, emptying another drawer. "Diana, sort these out and put them over there. Yes, I often stayed there. It was the funniest little seaside village you ever could imagine then. Only a few shops, no pier, no promenade, a few cottages—and the old inn. You'll never guess what it was called!"

"Rubadub Inn?" said Roger.

"No. It was called Three Men in a Tub!" said Miss Pepper "You know the old rhyme—'Rubadub-dub, Three men in a tub.' Goodness knows why the inn should have been named that, but it was—and still is. Actually Rubadub village was called that because of a strange whirlpool place set between some queer-shaped rocks. One is like a scrubbing-board, and down below it the water boils and swirls and bubbles. . . ."

"As if it were in a wash-tub, I suppose!" said Diana. "Rubadub, See how we scrub . . ."

"That's right," said Miss Pepper. "The whirlpool is called Rubadub Pool, and so the village got its name, I suppose."

"It sounds jolly good," said Snubby approvingly. "I like the sound of all this, I must say. An inn called Three Men in a Tub, and a whirlpool called Rubadub Pool—I say, do we stay at the inn, Miss Pepper?"

"We do," said Miss Pepper. "I stayed there as a child and it was very comfortable. My niece stayed there last year and she sent such good accounts of it that when your mother suggested somewhere for you all these holidays, I thought of Rubadub."

"It'll be nice to stay in a dear little old-fashioned seaside village," said Diana. "No pier, no promenade, no . . ."

"Oh yes, there's a pier now *and* a promenade, and plenty of things going on," said Miss Pepper briskly. "And there's an enormous Secret Harbour built there, too, round beyond Rubadub Pool—where new submarines are tried out. Oh, Rubadub is no longer a tiny, sleepy village!"

"I say! A Secret Harbour!" said Snubby, thrilled. "I should like to go over that."

"I said 'Secret'," said Miss Pepper. " 'Top Secret' too, Snubby. So well guarded that no one, not even an inquisitive lad like you, could possibly get near it. So get that out of your head."

There came a call from downstairs. "Miss Pepper! Can you come? There are a few things I want you to do."

"Coming, Mrs. Lynton!" called Miss Pepper, and hurried out of the room. Loony immediately jumped up to go with her and leapt after her, quite forgetting he was tied to the bed-rail by his lead. He almost choked himself.

"It all sounds super," said Snubby, comforting poor Loony. "I'm sorry Aunt Susan's not coming, though. But I don't mind if Uncle Richard doesn't. Sooner or later I always seem to get a whacking from him."

"You got two, last hols," said Diana. "One for letting Loony chew up his best slippers, and one for cheeking him."

"Don't remind me," said Snubby. "I have to think twice now before I say anything to Uncle Richard in case he might think I am cheeking him. It's an awful nuisance."

"It's a jolly good thing," said Roger. "You want keeping down, young Snubby. And while you're about it, you can think twice before you cheek me, too. Oh, blow you, Loony—how did you get those swim-suits off the bed?"

A loud sound rang through the house, and the three

children and Loony gave cries of joy. "The gong! I thought it was never going!"

"Race you downstairs! Come on, Loony!"

And down went an avalanche at top speed. Mr. Lynton groaned. "How *pleased* I shall be to see the coast of quiet, peaceful America. This house is Bedlam—never a moment's peace anywhere!"

CHAPTER TWO

GETTING READY

MR. AND MRS. LYNTON were to set off in their car after the meal. Everything was ready. The cases were packed and labelled. Big *Queen Elizabeth* labels were tied on, or pasted on. The tickets were safely in Mr. Lynton's wallet.

He was smiling as he said good-bye. He shook hands with Miss Pepper. "Don't stand any nonsense," he said to her. "And keep Snubby in his place. We'll write from New York. You've got our hotel address, haven't you?"

"Yes, thank you," said Miss Pepper. "Have a good time, and don't worry about the children. They'll be quite safe with me down at Rubadub. I'll see they don't get into mischief."

"No mysteries, please, and no adventures," said Mrs. Lynton, kissing her old governess. "Keep an eye on that, won't you—you know what extraordinary things can happen when these three are together."

"Good-bye, Mother! Don't forget to write!"

"Good-bye, Aunt Susan! I hope you don't get a storm that wrecks you!"

"Good-bye—and we'll be very good, so you needn't worry."

"Where's Loony?" said Snubby suddenly. "He wants to say good-bye too. Where on earth is he? Loony, Loony, Loony!"

"He *doesn't* want to say good-bye," said Miss Pepper firmly. "I've shut him in my bedroom."

The Lyntons got into the car. Snubby gave a yell and pointed up to Miss Pepper's bedroom window. Loony was there, his head squeezed through the half-open window, trying his best to see what was happening. He gave a bark.

"He did want to say good-bye!" cried Snubby. "Bark, Loony, bark!"

By a great effort Loony managed to push up the window a little way, and out came his shoulders and one paw.

"That dog will jump out next!" cried Mr. Lynton and jammed down the accelerator. The car leapt forward and was off down the road. Mr. Lynton had no desire to see Loony leap out of a high window!

Snubby tore upstairs and was just in time to stop Loony from flinging himself out of the window. "That dog!" said Miss Pepper, as they all went back to the house. "I can't imagine what the people at the inn will say about him. They said they didn't mind dogs—but they don't know Loony! Does he still go for brushes and mats?"

"Oh yes—and since he went to stay with your sister's dog, Loopy, last May, when we all went away with you after 'flu, he's taken to bringing down all the towels too," said Diana. "He caught that from Loopy."

"Well, we'll simply *have* to stop him doing things like that at the inn," said Miss Pepper, having a sudden vision of Loony piling all the visitors' towels out in the inn's garden, and then going back to fetch hair-brushes to put with them.

"I don't see how we *can* stop him," said Roger. "You simply can't reason with Loony. He just sits and grins at you with his tongue out, and thumps his tail on the floor. But you do love him, don't you, Miss Pepper?"

"I feel doubtful about that sometimes," said Miss Pepper. "Very doubtful. Now we'll all have to get very busy indeed, Roger and Diana, if we're going to be ready to go to-morrow. You'll have to help me pack."

Loony came trotting down the stairs looking very pleased with himself. For once he had no brush or towel with him. Snubby followed.

"We're going for a walk," he announced.

"Oh no you're not," said Roger at once. "Trust you to try and get out of fetching and carrying, Snubby—and lugging heavy cases about. You're jolly well going to stay here and help."

"I'd much rather Snubby took Loony for a walk," said Miss Pepper hastily, thinking it would be marvellous to get both boy and dog out of the way together. "I'm sure Loony needs a walk."

"Pah!" said Roger in disgust. "Snubby always gets out of everything."

"Go along, Snubby—but be back by teatime," said Miss Pepper firmly, and Snubby went, followed by his faithful and adoring Loony, his long black ears flopping as he went—pad-pad-pad-pad.

The others spent a busy afternoon. Everything was packed. Diana neatly wrote a dozen labels, Roger tied rope round the trunk.

"I'll help you down the stairs with that," said Miss Pepper. "I've just got to find Diana's sandals to put into this last bag."

Roger didn't want any help. He prided himself on his strength, and while Miss Pepper was hunting for the missing sandals, he dragged the trunk to the top of the stairs.

He set it flat and gave it a push. It cascaded down the stairs with a thunderous noise, arriving in the hall at top speed. Sardine the cat got the fright of her life as the trunk rumbled past where she sat on the stairs, waiting to pounce on someone coming down. She leapt in the air, and then tore like a streak of lightning into Diana's bedroom, as Miss Pepper was coming out in a hurry. Sardine shot between her ankles and landed on the bed, all her fur standing on end and her tail twice its usual size.

Miss Pepper rushed out on the landing. "Oh, who's fallen downstairs! Are you hurt? Whatever's happened?"

The cook was standing in the hall, brought out of her kitchen by the noise. She looked in disgust at the trunk, which had slid along the polished floor to the front door.

"Starting to throw trunks at one another now, I suppose," she said, and stalked back to her kitchen.

"What's the matter?" asked Roger, surprised. "I just shot the trunk downstairs, that's all. Jolly good idea—no lifting or carrying. I thought it would save us trouble, Miss Pepper."

Miss Pepper gave him such a glare that he disappeared into his room. Without a word she walked back to Diana's room, and picked up some socks.

"For two pins I'd leave them to themselves!" she thought, her heart still beating in fright. "Really, if Roger starts doing things like this my life won't be worth living. Snubby's bad enough."

Roger came humbly into the room. "I'm sorry, Miss Pepper," he said. "I didn't know it would crash down like that. Let me take those cases. I can carry them down for you one by one. You have a rest now, do."

"It's all right," said Miss Pepper thinking that the three children had their nice ways after all. "But I do wish you'd remember that you're in your teens, Roger, and be a bit more responsible."

"You sound like my form-master," said Roger gloomily. "Don't preach, Miss Pepper. You're too nice to preach."

Miss Pepper laughed and pretended to box Roger's ears. He ducked, grinning. He was very fond of her, as they all were, and hated it when she was vexed.

At last everything was finished. It was teatime and

Snubby arrived back punctually with a tired Loony and an enormous appetite. He went straight into the kitchen to find the plump, good-natured cook.

"Cookie! Have you made any of your gingerbread for me? Don't say you haven't! I've been thinking of it all the term."

"Go on with you," said the cook. She opened the larder door and took out a tin. She lifted the lid and showed Snubby a great flat slab of sticky-looking home-made gingerbread. He gave her a hug round her waist.

"You're my very best friend," he said. "You don't mind if we eat it all, do you? I mean—it's a real compliment, really, if we eat up every single crumb. Isn't it, Cookie dear?"

"Go on with you!" said the cook again. "You'd talk the hind leg off a donkey, you would!"

"Why, is one of your legs coming loose?" inquired Snubby at once, and dodged out of the way as the cook took up a frying-pan and threatened him with it. Snubby's silly jokes usually went down very well with the good-tempered cook, and Mrs. Lynton always said that they had more and better cakes when Snubby was with them than at any other time.

"It's a wonder I did any work at all this afternoon," said the cook, taking the gingerbread carefully out of the tin. "That cousin of yours threw trunks down the stairs, and my word, they made a noise. I nearly had a heart attack!"

"Oh I say—good old Roger!" said Snubby, breaking a bit off the end of the gingerbread. "Strong man he's getting, isn't he? Wish I'd been there to see him throwing trunks all over the place."

"Now take your fingers away from my gingerbread," said the cook. "And take that dog out of my kitchen. I never in my life knew any animal that could slink into the larder when the door's shut, like that dog of yours can. He's a living miracle!"

"He is. You're right," said Snubby, wholeheartedly. "I'm glad you appreciate him. Oh golly, here's Sardine. We'd better go."

They left hurriedly. Sardine considered that the kitchen belonged to her, and hissed and spat spitefully if Loony stayed too long!

Teatime passed very pleasantly, because there were hot scones and honey, and gingerbread and some coconut buns. After that they all tidied up their rooms and put away everything. Loony helped by gathering together all the loose mats and putting them in a pile on the landing for people to fall over.

"I really think it's about time for Loony to grow up a bit," said Diana, picking herself up after stumbling over the mats in the darkness of the landing. "He's nearly two years old, and reckoning that in human years, it means he's in his teens. He ought to be more re*spon*sible."

Roger grinned at Miss Pepper nearby. "Another preacher!" he said. "Loony, do you hear what Di says?"

"What's the time?" said Miss Pepper, looking at her watch. "It's gone eight. I think you'd all better go to bed now We've got a long day before us to-morrow. I want a bit of peace and quiet, too, to write letters."

"All right—we'll go," said Diana. "I always think it's thrilling, the night before we go away. Thinking about the sea and bathing and prawning, and walks. . . ."

"Woof!" said Loony, at once. He always joined in the conversation when he heard that word.

"Clever dog!" said Diana. "Come on—let's all go to bed."

CHAPTER THREE

OFF TO RUBADUB-ON-SEA

THE NEXT day was truly exciting. Usually the three children went off for their holidays by car, but they much preferred the train.

They found an empty carriage, and each bagged a corner. Looney shared everyone's corner in turn, breathing down their necks in excitement.

It was a long way to Woodlingham, where they had to change trains. The journey was a cross-country one, involving many long stops at various stations at which bits and pieces of the train were added or subtracted.

Snubby, of course, was intensely interested in these stops, and talked to every engine-driver, guard and porter that he could see.

"Do you know," he announced once, as he returned from a chat to the driver, "do you know that of all the fifteen carriages we started with, only two of the original ones are left now—ours and the next one? Such a lot have been shunted off. But some have been added, of course."

"You make it sound like a maths problem," said Diana. "So long as they leave our carriage on the train that's all I care about."

"Just like a girl," said Roger scornfully. "No interest in railways at all. I call it all very thrilling. We start with fifteen—we shunted off six at Limming and added five. We left another three at Berklemere, and got two more added on at Fingerpit. Now let me see. . . ."

"This sounds like a riddle now," said Miss Pepper sleepily. "If we shunt off six and add two, and leave five somewhere, and forget to take on the rest, please tell me the name of the engine-driver!"

"Ha, ha, joke," said Snubby politely. "I say, isn't it time for lunch yet?"

They got to Woodlingham at last and woke up Miss Pepper, who had fallen sound asleep. "It's a good thing we're *respons*ible people," said Roger. "*Some*body's got to look out for the station we change at."

"Don't be idiotic, Roger," said Miss Pepper. "I can't imagine how I could have gone to sleep in this rattling, rumbling old train."

The train to take them to Rockypool came in at last. Snubby went to talk to the engine-driver, having found out that there was a ten-minute wait before it drew out of the station again.

He didn't notice that another engine came backing up to the end of the train. He didn't notice it being hooked on. He suddenly heard the whistle of the guard and the voices of the others calling him frantically.

"Snubby, quick, we're going. SNUBBY!"

Snubby leapt into the very last carriage, dragging poor Loony in by his collar. "Gosh!" he said to a surprised old country-woman there. "I nearly missed it! How was I to know the thing was going to go off the other way? Peculiar way trains behave here!"

"Ar," said the old woman wisely.

"I mean—it came in with the engine at the front, just as usual—and it leaves the station with a perfectly fresh

16

engine, at the *back*," said Snubby, working himself up into a grievance because he felt so foolish. It's time somebody spoke about these things."

"Ar," said the old lady, nodding her head. Snubby looked at her. In his experience people who said nothing but "Ar" made extremely good listeners. So he aired his views at great length and enjoyed himself thoroughly. He didn't even get out at the next station or the next, to find his way to the carriage where the others were. He was afraid they would tease him unmercifully about being so nearly left behind.

Two men got in at the third station. Snubby looked at them closely. They were naval men, he saw. Aha! Probably they belonged to the Secret Submarine Harbour. What a scoop for him if he could make friends with them and get news of the harbour to retell proudly to the others. The men opened newspapers and began to read.

"Excuse me, sir, but are we very far from Rockypool?" began Snubby. "I've got to get out there."

"You'll see the name of the station when we come to it," said one of the men gruffly.

"I say, sir, I suppose you don't belong to the Secret Submarine place, do you?" Snubby tried again. "I've always been interested in submarines. Used to sail them in my bath, and . . ."

"You probably do still, I imagine," said the other man. "Shut up!"

Snubby subsided, grieved. He examined the men carefully pretending he was a detective. Both clean-shaven. One with a mole on his right cheek. One with crooked eyebrows. Actually he thought they looked nice men. It was a pity they wouldn't talk. He sat and stared at them thoughtfully.

"Anything wrong with my face?" inquired one man at last. "What about looking out of the window for a change?"

Snubby scowled. He woke up Loony, who was sound asleep under the seat, bored with this long journey. He lugged him up on the seat and began to talk to him. He couldn't very well talk to the old woman, because she was now snoring in her corner, her mouth wide open.

"Shut up!" said one of the men again. "What a babbler you are!"

The old woman woke up unexpectedly. She gave a little wheeze of laughter.

"That's right, he is," she said. "Babbles like a brook, he do. I couldn't get a word in till you come along, misters."

Snubby glared at her indignantly. He got out at the next station with much dignity, and made his way to the compartment where Roger and Diana were hanging out of the window.

"Why didn't you come before?" demanded Roger. "Was there somebody interesting in that carriage?"

"Rather!" said Snubby, climbing in. "There were two men from the Secret Submarine place—and my word, the secrets they know!"

"As if they'd tell *you* any!" said Roger at once.

"All right. If you're feeling like that I won't tell you a word," said Snubby exasperatingly. He sat down in the opposite corner. Roger stared at him. He couldn't believe that any one would tell Snubby anything interesting in the way of secrets—but on the other hand Snubby was so friendly that people *had* been known to relate most amazing bits of information to him.

"Go on—tell me what you heard," said Roger. "Who were the men? What were they like?"

"They wouldn't tell me their names," said Snubby. "So I didn't press them. But I can tell you exactly what they were like. You just never know when it'll pay you to be really observant."

He described the men exactly, down to a mole, crooked eyebrows, two overlapping teeth, bitten nails on one man's hands, and misshapen little finger on the other man's.

"Jolly good," said Roger, thinking for the hundredth time that his fat-headed little cousin could be quite sharp, for all his idiotic ways. "You ought to go into the police force!"

Snubby was about to air his views on how lucky the police force would be to get him, when the train slowed down at a station.

"Rockypool!" yelled a porter, and Miss Pepper stood up quickly.

"Ah—here we are. Roger, go and see if our trunks and cases are *still* in the luggage van. I can hardly believe we have the same luggage van as when we started, but still, you never know!"

Roger disappeared to find out. Snubby and Diana handed down the smaller cases and parcels, and they all got out of the carriage. Loony got his lead entangled round Snubby's legs as usual, and made him cross.

Roger came back. "The luggage is all there," he announced. "Safe as can be. What about a taxi, Miss Pepper? Shall I go and see if there's one?"

"It's already ordered," said Miss Pepper. "I asked the innkeeper's wife at Rubadub to order one for us. It should be waiting."

It was. As they walked to it Snubby nudged Roger and nodded his head towards two men walking nearby. Roger looked at them and immediately recognised a good many of the big and small characteristics that Snubby had recited to him. He stared at the men with interest. Like Snubby he thought it must be thrilling to work on anything secret.

Their taxi was waiting. The driver got down to help the porter in with their things. He strapped on the trunk, and put the cases in front.

"Is it far to Rubadub?" asked Snubby. The man shook his head.

"Matter of three miles," he said. "The railway don't go any farther than this."

They all got into the old musty-smelling taxi. Snubby stuck his head out of the window to take a look round. The country they passed through was rather wild and desolate—heath and moorland with pools of water shining here and there.

They rumbled along. Snubby looked at Loony anxiously.

"I think he's going to be sick," he said.

"Oh no!" said Miss Pepper, in despair.

"He'd better go in front with the driver," said Snubby, and he knocked on the glass. "Hey—stop a minute, will you? I'm coming in front with you."

The taxi stopped. Snubby got out, carrying Loony, who looked very surprised. The two of them were soon in front with the driver, sitting on a pile of cases.

"Now I can see fine," said Snubby to the driver, and grinned happily.

"Well I never!" said Diana, who heard this. "I bet

Loony wasn't feeling sick after all. It was just that Snubby wanted to sit in front and see everything."

"Well, never mind," said Miss Pepper, who was feeling tired, and not very anxious to cope with the inexhaustible and irrepressible Snubby. "We'll soon be there."

It didn't seem long before the taxi drove into a little town by the sea. It was set in a semi-circle of cliff, looking out to a small bay. There was a good promenade, a fine little pier, a stone jetty with boats and a sandy beach.

"It looks grand!" said Diana, pleased. "And oh, look —is this lovely old place the inn?"

"Yes—this is the Three Men in a Tub Inn, in the old town of Rubadub!" said Miss Pepper. "Out you get— we're here at last!"

CHAPTER FOUR

THE QUEER OLD INN

THEY ALL tumbled out of the taxi. The driver gave a shout to someone called by the queer name of Dummy.

"Hey there, Dummy! Come and collect these things, will you? Your people have arrived."

The children stood and looked at the Three Men in a Tub Inn. It had an old, old sign, but whether it was of three men in a tub, or of anything else it was quite impossible to tell, it was so dark and dingy.

The inn looked like something out of a story. "If you told me we were back in the Middle Ages I'd believe you!" said Diana, staring up at the inn. "I feel as if I've gone back hundreds of years when I look at this quaint old place!"

It was a rambling old inn, set back against the cliff, almost nestling into it. Its leaded, diamond-paned windows gleamed brightly. It had tall chimneys, and a roof so covered with grey-green lichen that the red tiles only showed through here and there.

The front door might have belonged to a castle! It was enormous, very stout and strong, and had a great knocker in the form of a sailing ship. Snubby, of course immediately wanted to go and bang on it, but before he could do so the old door creaked open and a face looked out with round eyes and a button of a mouth.

At first the children thought it was the face of a child, but when the whole person appeared they saw that it was a grown-up! A grown-up not as tall as Roger, the head rather big for the body, and the face an odd mixture of child and grown-up.

"Come on, Dummy. Stir yourself," said the driver, undoing some of the cases. Dummy ran out clumsily. He wore the dress of a hall-porter or odd-man—thick, navy-blue trousers with a line down the side, a leather apron and waistcoat over a dark shirt. He grinned at the children, holding his face sideways as if half-shy.

He appeared to be enormously strong! He lifted the trunk with ease, jerked it on his shoulder, and went back into the inn with it.

"That's old Dummy," explained the taxi-driver. "He's a good chap, but never properly growed-up, I don't reckon. Strong as a horse, and gentle as a child—unless he gets into one of his rages, and then all I say is, I'd rather meet a lion than Dummy!"

"I liked him," said Diana. "He had a nice sort of smile."

"He gets on well with children," said the taxi-driver. "But when grown-ups go for him for being a bit slow, like, he mutters and mumbles and growls and scowls, and looks as if he'd like to throw them over the cliff. And see you don't ever laugh at old Dummy. Anyone who laughs at Dummy comes to a sticky end, so I've been told."

Miss Pepper thought that the taxi-driver had talked quite enough. She saw Snubby drinking in every word, eager to ask about the people who "had come to a sticky end."

"I think that's all," she said, taking out her purse. "Thank you for meeting us."

The driver touched his cap, and pocketed the fare and the generous tip that Miss Pepper had given him. Then he drove away.

Dummy appeared again to take the rest of the cases, and brought with him the innkeeper's wife. She was a large, plump woman with rather a gloomy face. She had so many chins that Snubby was quite lost in admiration. She did her hair high up on her head, and really looked rather majestic.

"Good afternoon," she said, advancing on the little company. "Your train must have been very punctual for once in a way. It's usually so late that I didn't expect you for another half-hour. Come this way. Your rooms are all ready."

"Oh, thank you, Mrs. er—Mrs. . . . ." said Miss Pepper, rather taken aback by the ponderous plumpness of the innkeeper's wife.

"My name is Glump," said that lady. "Mrs. Glump."

"What a wonderful name!" murmured Diana, as they all went into the big, dark hall, following Mrs. Glump. "And doesn't it suit her?"

"Yes—mixture of 'glum' and 'plump,' " said Snubby with a giggle. "I wonder if there are any little Glumps. Come on—up the stairs we go. My word, aren't they uneven and steep?"

"Mind the bends," said Mrs. Glump, in her stately voice. "Oh my—what's that?"

It was only Loony, escaped from Snubby's hand, tearing up the stairs, pressing himself against her legs as he passed her at sixty miles an hour. He liked this place. He knew he would find plenty of strange, unusual smells here.

"I'm so sorry—did he scare you?" said Snubby in his politest voice. "That was only my spaniel. He's excited because he's come to a new place. You don't mind dogs, do you? Miss Pepper said you took dogs."

"I take *well-behaved* dogs," said Mrs. Glump, leading them down a twisting corridor, lined with stout old doors. "I have a dog of my own, very well trained and most obedient."

"What's his name?" asked Roger.

"We call him Mr. Tubby, short for Three Men in a Tub," said Mrs. Glump. "My husband's idea of a joke. It took me a very long time to see it. But now that he—the dog, I mean—is old and fat, I must say that his name suits him very well."

She went up a few more stairs and came to a small square landing, out of which opened four or five doors.

"This is where I have put you," she said, and opened one of the doors. "This is the best of the rooms. Perhaps Miss Pepper would like it."

"Oh, I *should*!" said Miss Pepper in delight. "I once had it when I stayed here as a child. Oh, the view—it's exactly the same as it always was!"

She went to the leaded casement window and flung it wide open. The children crowded beside her.

The room looked out down a steep cliffside to the golden sands below. The sea was cornflower blue that August day, and the sound of the waves below came softly up to the window.

"Like someone sighing," said Diana to herself. "But I expect on a stormy day the noise of the waves would be terrific. Oh, I hope my room has the same view as this!"

It had. It was a much smaller room with a queer slanting ceiling. Big beams ran crookedly across the walls, which were whitewashed. There was almost the same view as from Miss Pepper's room, but a little farther west.

The boys pronounced their room to be "smashingly super," and called Diana to see it. It was a big room with

23

a built-in oak cupboard, an old double bed that looked as if it had once been a four-poster but had had its four upright posts taken off, and a very uneven floor that would trip the boys up hundreds of times before their visit was over!

"This place has got a lovely old *feel*," said Diana. "Don't you think so, boys?"

"Rather," said Roger. "Like Hampton Court or the Tower or somewhere frightfully old. You can feel that things have happened here for years—the walls still remember them!"

"Funny. I feel like that too," said Snubby, rather astonished. "And I feel this has been a happy place, too—enormous meals and things."

"You *would* think that," said Diana. "If the walls could talk to you, all you'd want them to tell you about would be the meals people had downstairs."

"I wouldn't mind having a meal now," said Snubby. "Do we unpack? Where's Miss Pepper?"

Miss Pepper came in to see what the boys' room was like. She immediately shooed Loony off the big bed. "Snubby, you heard what Mrs. Glump said about well-behaved dogs, didn't you?" she said. "For goodness' sake tell Loony he can't behave here as if he was at home. Mrs. Glump would have plenty to say."

"It's a marvellous name, Glump," said Snubby. "Sort of gloomy and gluggy and gurgley and . . ."

"Oh, don't be *silly*, Snubby," said Miss Pepper. "Hurry up and unpack and come down to tea. Mrs. Glump said it would be ready when you are."

"Well, I am now," said Snubby at once.

"No, you're not. You've got to wash yourself and brush your hair—it's like a red-haired mop—and for goodness' sake brush your shorts too. You look as if you've been scrambling about under all the carriage seats on the train."

"I shall go all gloomy and glumpish if you scold me as soon as we get here," complained Snubby. "I feel glumpish already."

Diana gave a little squeal of laughter. "Oh, Snubby—that's a lovely word. Much better than gloomy. Do you feel down in the glumps?"

"Not really," grinned Snubby. "Hey, Loony, get off that bed. Didn't you hear what pepper-pot said?"

"You'll get into trouble with Miss Pepper if you begin calling her that," said Roger. "She won't stand cheek from you. I say, it's a shame our room doesn't look out over the sea, isn't it?"

"Yes. But it's got quite an *interesting* view," said Snubby, looking out of the small casement window. Chimneys and roofs and other people's windows."

It was rather a peculiar view, really. Their part of the inn was higher than the other part, and they could see across uneven roofs and into attic windows here and there. They could see tall chimneys rising up too, one of them with wisps of smoke coming out.

"I wouldn't mind exploring this roof some time," said Snubby, washing his face vigorously. "I'm good at exploring roofs. You never know when that kind of thing comes in useful."

"You're an awful fathead, Snubby," said Roger. "Look, that dog's on the bed again. I think really it would be best to drape it with an old rug or something. I don't see *how* we're to keep Loony off it. Come on, Loony—teatime."

They called Diana and Miss Pepper, and went down the twisting, uneven stairs, moving rather cautiously because of the sharp bends in the stairway where one side of the stairs narrowed to an inch or two. Loony, of course, missed his footing and fell headlong down, bouncing merrily from stair to stair.

"Can't you behave, Loony!" hissed Snubby. "*WHAT* will Mr. Tubby think of you?"

CHAPTER FIVE

AFTER TEA

THEY HAD tea in the dining-room of the inn. This was a large, rather dark room, with heavy oak beams across the ceilings and walls. It had a colossal fireplace, now filled with foxgloves, and an amazing number of doors, all polished oak.

Snubby saw that the tea was good and fell upon it ravenously. New brown bread and butter and home-made damson jam disappeared down his throat without stopping.

"You're a greedy pig, Snubby," said Diana. "You get worse instead of better. I say, isn't this a heavenly room? It's got stags' heads all round, and big glass cases of fish. And look at those funny old prints—and did you ever see such a selection of horse-brasses hanging down each side of the mantelpiece?"

"Horse-brasses?" said Snubby, pausing in his munching. "I say—I collect those. I must have a look at them and see if there are any I haven't got."

"Ass! You've got about nine, that's all, and there must be seventy or eighty there," said Diana. "Look at that old clock, too, Snubby. It's enormous."

It was an old grandfather clock, the biggest the children had ever seen in their lives. It almost reached the ceiling, and its tick was so loud that it could be heard all over the room—TICK-TOCK, TICK-TOCK. When five o'clock came it burst into the loudest dong-dong-dongs that the children had ever heard, except from Big Ben. It was quite deafening.

"Miss Pepper, is everything just like it was when you came here as a child?" asked Roger. "Was that clock there then? Do you remember it?"

"Oh yes—and I remember someone hiding inside the big pendulum case at the bottom once, and frightening the life out of me by growling inside there like a dog," said Miss Pepper rashly. Snubby had already pricked up his ears at this idea, of course.

"That's a smashing idea," he said at once. "I'll remember that."

"No, don't," said Miss Pepper, with a groan. "Please, Snubby, behave yourself here. I'm almost sure I knew Mrs. Glump as a child, and I don't want her to put you down as a lot of hooligans and think that I can't manage you all."

"Gosh—did you really know Mrs. Glump when she was a girl?" asked Snubby in wonder. "Was she older than you?"

"About the same age," said Miss Pepper. "She was a funny shy little girl then. See—what was her name now—oh yes—Gloria."

"Gloria Glump!" exclaimed Diana, in delight. "It can't be true."

"Sh!" said Miss Pepper, afraid that Mrs. Glump might hear Diana. "She wasn't Glump then. Her name was Gloria Tregonnan, as far as I remember. Her family have had this inn for hundreds of years so it's said."

Mrs. Glump suddenly appeared at the door. "Have you enough tea?" she inquired in her ponderous voice. "Oh dear—why, there's hardly anything left. Er—shall I send in some more?"

"No, thank you," said Miss Pepper, feeling suddenly certain that a good part of the tea had gone under the table to a ravenous Loony. That must have been why he had been so very quiet! She frowned at Snubby, who was just opening his mouth to protest that *he* could do with some more to eat. He shut it again.

"Now, while I unpack, you can go and explore the beach," she said. "And if it's wet, please tie your sand-shoes round your neck. You hear me, Snubby?"

They rushed off. Miss Pepper poured herself out another cup of tea and drank it quietly. Mrs. Glump reappeared.

"Handful, aren't they?" she said sympathetically. "My, children aren't what they were in our day, are they? We had to be seen and not heard."

"They're not bad children at all," said Miss Pepper loyally. "A bit high-spirited at times. Are you very full now, Mrs. Glump—many visitors here?"

"Well, we're not over-full at the moment," said Mrs. Glump. "There's a big new hotel built down in the town now, you know—near to the pier—and that's taken a lot of my custom away. We're old-fashioned here at Three Men in a Tub, and a bit out of the way."

Miss Pepper looked at one or two tables with napkins folded by the plates, and dishes of fruit. "You seem to have a few visitors besides ourselves," she said.

"Oh yes—I've two or three of the pierrots staying here," said Mrs. Glump. "There's a very good pierrot show on the pier every night, you know. They call themselves 'The Rubadub Rollicks,' whatever that may mean. 'Come to the Rubadub Rollicks for a Rollicking Show,' is on posters all over the place."

"Oh, the children will like to go and see them," said Miss Pepper. "Is there a funny man?"

"Oh yes—very funny," said Mrs. Glump. "They'll love him. He's staying here, as a matter of fact. And there's a

27

conjurer too—queer thing to have in a pierrot show, but he goes down quite well, I believe. He's here too—and Miss Iris Nightingale, the singer from the show. That's not her real name, of course, she chose it because it's a good name for a singer."

"You've got some quite interesting people," said Miss Pepper, enjoying the chat. "Anyone else?"

"Well, there's an old fellow called Professor James," said Mrs. Glump. "I would like you to warn the children not to upset him, please, Miss Pepper. He doesn't like dogs, not even my well-trained Mr. Tubby. He's rather deaf, and he's got a very hot temper."

Miss Pepper made a mental note to warn all the children, especially Snubby, and to keep Loony strictly under control when Professor James was about.

"And there's Miss Twitt," said Mrs. Glump. "That's the lot. She's all right, but she's what I call a *gusher*. Gushes over children and dogs and cats and the pretty butterflies and the darling birds, and all that. I wouldn't want the children to laugh at her."

"Oh dear!" thought Miss Pepper. "I hope they won't. I'll have to give them quite a talking to to-night."

She told Mrs. Glump how, long ago, she had known her as a shy little girl, and the innkeeper's wife nodded her head in pleasure. Well, well—to think she and Miss Pepper had known each other as girls!

"The inn is very little changed!" said Miss Pepper. "I shall love being here again!"

She went up to unpack. She looked at the glorious view from the little window and sat down to enjoy it. It all looked so very peaceful and serene! What a lovely quiet part of the world this was!

Just as she got up again, a muffled explosion shook the inn. Miss Pepper sat down again suddenly, feeling scared. What in the world was that?

She went out on the landing, feeling alarmed. Dummy was there, carrying somebody's case. He grinned shyly at her.

"What was that awful noise?" asked Miss Pepper.

"Boom-boom-boom," said Dummy, delighted. He put down the case with a crash that made Miss Pepper jump. "BOOM!" he said, and did it again.

"Don't," said Miss Pepper. "I just wanted to know what made that loud noise."

Dummy took Miss Pepper by the arm and led her to a little door. Behind it was a stairway. It led steeply upwards. He went up it and beckoned Miss Pepper. In surprise, she followed. The staircase led up to the roof, through a small trap-door which had a piece of glass set in it, like a small skylight.

"Boom-boom," said Dummy softly, pulling Miss Pepper beside him, their heads sticking out of the skylight trap-door.

She was now so high that she was almost on a level with the top of the cliff behind the hotel, where it suddenly slanted downwards. There was a deep cleft in it at one place, and the skylight opening looked directly through the cleft to the sea on the other side of the cliff.

It was surprising to see right over the cliff to the sea away on the other side. Miss Pepper gazed curiously. She remembered that the Secret Submarine base was somewhere over there, closely guarded on all sides, land and sea. Experiments, top-secret experiments, went on there. Perhaps the muffled explosion she had heard came from one of these experiments.

"Booooom-ooom!" The far-away noise made her jump again. Before the noise came she had seen a little cloud of either smoke or spray rising from the sea on the other side of the cliff. The noise made her certain it was an explosion of some sort.

"Boom-boom," said Dummy, who seemed quite unable to say anything else, pointing and grinning.

"Yes. Very interesting. Thank you, Dummy," said Miss Pepper. Dummy gave her his engaging sideways smile, and his bright blue eyes looked shyly at her. She patted him on the arm. What a queer little man he was—more like a gnome or brownie than a human being!

She made up her mind to tell the children what she had seen when they came home. They would be thrilled! She went to unpack once more, humming. The weeks seemed to stretch away before her, full of sunshine and walks and reading, and looking after three interesting madcaps of children.

They were having a lovely time by themselves. They had explored the sandy beach, which was studded with hundreds of pinkish shells. They had climbed a few rocks, and Snubby had slipped into a pool and sat down heavily. Now he dripped water wherever he went.

They went down the promenade, and came to the pier, where they examined all the notices.

"'Come to the Rubadub Rollicks for a Rollicking Show,'" said Roger, reading the biggest poster. "I say, we ought to go and see them. I love pierrots. Look, it says there's a conjurer too. Matthew Marvels. We'll have to go and see *him*!"

They examined the photographs of the twelve pierrots. The children thought they looked fine.

"So long as the girls don't *sing* too much," said Snubby. "An awful waste of time when you've got a conjurer and a funny man as well. I don't mind the dancing so much—but all that singing's boring."

"Loony's gone on the pier," said Roger suddenly. "Loony, come back! Loony, Loony!"

Loony was half-way down the pier. He took absolutely no notice of the shouts. He had smelt an enticing fishy smell somewhere at the end of the pier and he was going to examine it if it was very last thing he did.

"We'll have to spend tuppence and fetch him," said Snubby in disgust. "Anyone got tuppence?"

"Yes. *You* have!" said Roger. "You don't get tuppence out of me that way. Spend your own pence on your own dog."

So Snubby had to fork out tuppence and go and yank a disappointed Loony out of a pile of decaying fish at the very end of the pier.

"Can't you hear the seagulls yelling at you, idiot?" said Snubby severely. "That's put there for them. What a dog you are! Can't even understand the rude names the gulls are calling you!"

CHAPTER SIX

THE OTHER GUESTS

THEY GOT back to the inn about seven o'clock. Miss Pepper had said they must be in by then because the inn served dinner, and everyone was expected to come in on time for that.

"You *are* nice and early," she said, hearing them come up on the landing, and going to her door to greet them. "Did you have a good look round?"

"Rather! It's a super place," said Roger. "Did you hear any bangs, Miss Pepper? We did, and a man told us they were from the Secret Submarine base. He says it's very hush-hush. I wish we could see over it."

"People don't see over hush-hush places," said Miss Pepper. "You might know that. Look, as you're in so early, I'll show you something. Dummy showed it to *me*."

She led the way to the door behind which was the little staircase. They all went up it wonderingly. Wherever did it lead to? Roger gave an exclamation when he reached the top and pushed up the trap-door to peer out.

"My word—we can see the Secret Base through that cleft in the cliff! How exciting!"

"Let me see!" said Snubby impatiently. "Di, do pull Loony down. He's pawing so hard at my shorts he'll make a hole in them. Gosh, Roger—what a view! I say, is that where the explosion came from Miss Pepper?"

"Yes. I actually saw the smoke—or spray, I think it must have been—from the second one," said Miss Pepper.

"I shall sit up here and watch for the third one," announced Snubby.

"No, you won't. You'll just come straight away down now," said Miss Pepper.

They all climbed down the little wooden stairway and went out of the door at the bottom, on to the landing. A man was just coming up to it from the lower stairs. He was a tall, thin man, with a long, cadaverous face, and deep-set, rather staring eyes. He looked in surprise at the children coming down the little stairway.

They stared back at him. Diana didn't like his eyes. She thought they seemed to look right through her, and she shivered. Who was he?

"Good evening," said Miss Pepper politely. She thought he must be one of the other guests.

"Good evening," said the man shortly, opened the door and disappeared into his room. He shut the door with a soft click.

Miss Pepper thought over the guests that Mrs. Glump had told her about, and came to the conclusion that the man could only be one of the pierrots who was staying there. Surely he wasn't the funny man, the comedian of the party? He didn't look as if he had ever laughed in his life. Then it must be Mr. Matthew Marvels, the conjurer. Well, he certainly looked more like a conjurer than a comedian!

"That must be Mr. Glooomp," whispered Snubby with a giggle. "Didn't he look the picture of gloom? Lost a shilling and found a farthing, I should think."

"Hurry up and change into something clean," said Miss Pepper. "And do remember that you have dinner here, not supper, and are supposed to look washed and brushed and tidy, and must put on your best manners."

"Oh dear," groaned Roger. "Is it that kind of place? Anyway, Snubby'll *have* to change. Look at the drips he's made on the landing already. He fell in a rock-pool."

"He would, of course," said Miss Pepper. "Snubby bring me your shorts to dry when you've changed into clean, dry ones."

When the gong boomed out over the house, the three children were all ready. Loony was too. "I've brushed him and washed the sand off him," said Snubby, proudly. "He looks fine, doesn't he? I want him to make a very good impression on Mr. Tubby Dog."

They were the first down in the dining-room. A most appetising smell of tomato soup came from the kitchen. Snubby sniffed loudly, and then caught Miss Pepper's eye.

A very portly dog waddled into the dining-room. He was enormous—a bull-mastiff with a most gloomy and lugubrious face, wrinkles and folds of flesh hanging down his cheeks.

"This must be Mr. Tubby," said Snubby, eyeing the big dog with awe. "I say—look at his wrinkles. Good evening, Mr. Tubby, let me introduce you to Loony. Mr. Tubby—Mr. Loony."

"Woof," said Loony, scared but polite.

"Grrrrr," said Mr. Tubby, and lifted the skin from his top teeth in a horrifying manner. Loony backed hurriedly into a waiter who was bringing in the soup.

Mr. Tubby walked to a rug by the fireplace and subsided there gradually, with a few rather human-sounding groans. He eyed everyone with a superior and contemptuous air, looking extremely miserable. Then he laid his great head on his paws and let out a sigh that blew along the floor like a draught.

Loony gazed at Mr. Tubby in awe. What a dog! What a grandfather of a dog! Loony felt extremely small and decided to behave himself. He lay down heavily on Snubby's feet.

The waiter laid plates of tomato soup in front of everyone. They had just begun when the other guests walked into the room. Miss Pepper glanced at them, recognising them from Mrs. Glump's description.

Mr. Marvels the conjurer came first. He was the man

they had met on the landing. Then came a man with a comical face, ears that stuck out and a broad smile. He winked across at the children, and joked with the waiter. He must be the funny man, decided Miss Pepper.

Then came a pretty girl of about twenty, who sat at the table with the conjurer and the funny man. She must be Iris Nightingale, the singer.

Finally came an old man with a beard, and a middle-aged lady fluttering with scarfs and bits of chiffon, and with a bow in her over-curled hair.

"Professor James—and Miss Twitt," thought Miss Pepper, drinking her soup. The children stared round at all the newcomers.

"Now," said the Professor, stopping just inside the room. "Where's that dog? Nowhere near my table, I hope."

Mr. Tubby didn't even deign to raise his head. Professor James stared at him with dislike and Mr. Tubby stared back sorrowfully and contemptuously.

"Ha! There you are!" said Professor James, advancing to his table. "Well, keep on the rug. Waiter, what soup is it?"

"Tomato, sir," said the waiter, a bright-eyed youth who had already exchanged a few winks with the irrepressible Snubby.

"What's that? Speak up, my man," said the Professor. "Everyone mumbles nowadays."

"Tomato, sir," said the waiter, a little more loudly.

"Bless the man—can't hear a word!" said the old fellow.

"He said 'TOMATO,' " said Snubby helpfully at the top of his voice. Everyone jumped violently including the Professor.

"Who's shouting?" said the Professor angrily. "Enough to deafen anyone!" He glared round at the children's table. Snubby got ready to confess at the top of his voice that it was he who had shouted, but Miss Pepper frowned so hard at him that he desisted.

"I should like some more tomato soup," he said in his normal voice.

A little laugh came to their ears. It was from Miss Twitt, who was sitting at the next table. She leaned over to Miss Pepper, one or two necklaces and bracelets jingling merrily.

34

"Isn't he *sweet*? Trying to be so helpful! And how nice to see such a healthy appetite!"

Snubby looked so completely horrified at being called "sweet" that Roger and Diana had to laugh.

"Such nice-looking children," gushed Miss Twitt. "Are you their mother?"

"No. I am merely in charge of them," said Miss Pepper, politely but coldly. Miss Twitt was the kind of person to avoid, she could see! She would rapidly drive the children to rudeness. "My name is Pepper. Miss Pepper."

"And mine is Twitt. Miss Twitt," was the reply. "We'll have to get together, Miss Pepper, when these rascals are safely in bed. I do *so* love children, don't you? *And* dogs, of course. Dear creatures!"

Loony decided to see who this gushing, talkative person was, and he appeared from below the table. This was the signal for a fresh outburst from Miss Twitt.

"Oh, the darling! Oh, I *do* love cockers! Come to me, my pet. I'll take you walky-walkies one day, shall I?"

Loony gave her one disgusted look and retired under the table. Mr. Tubby gave what sounded remarkably like a snigger, got up very slowly, and lay down on his rug with his back to Miss Twitt.

"And what are the children's names?" went on Miss Twitt, who could apparently talk and swallow hot soup at one and the same time. "What's the little girl's name?"

"I'm Diana. And I'm not a little girl," said Diana. "You sound as if you think I'm six!"

"I'm Roger," said Roger gruffly.

"And I'm Snubby, Miss Twitter," suddenly beamed Snubby. Diana gave a giggle.

"My name is Twitt, not Twitter," said Miss Twitt. "And how do you like Rubadub, children? Such a very quaint name, I always feel!"

"Yes, so *twee*, Miss Twitter," began Snubby. "Oh, what pretty dinky beads you wear, Miss Twitter."

"Snubby," said Miss Pepper, in such a fierce voice that he subsided at once. Miss Twitt looked at her in surprise.

"Get on with your meal, children, and don't let me hear another word," said Miss Pepper, afraid of the effect Miss Twitt would have on them if they entered into any lengthy conversation.

Snubby was really scared when Miss Pepper's voice

took on a certain tone. He began on a plate of cold chicken and ham and salad, unusually silent.

"Please, mayn't we talk now?" asked Diana after a while. "If we just talk to one another, I mean?"

Miss Twitt was now having an animated conversation with the funny man, who played up to her valiantly. Miss Pepper judged it was safe to let the three children use their tongues.

"Very well. But I've warned you," she said. "Don't go into the lounge after supper, please. Leave it to the other guests."

"Right. We'll all go for a walk then," said Roger. "*I* don't want to go into the lounge."

None of them did. Oh dear, thought Miss Pepper, this was going to be rather a *difficult* holiday!

CHAPTER SEVEN

FINE NEWS

THE THREE children and Loony set off once more for a quick walk. Miss Pepper had said it must only be a short one, as it was getting late. It was still light, of course—but as they turned down to the promenade they saw one of the buildings along it blazing with lights.

"It's a kind of fair," said Roger. "Let's go and have a squint at it."

"Oooh—it's got those Dodgem Cars," said Diana, thrilled. "Do you remember, we once had rides in them when somebody took us to a Play Camp. You kept crashing into me, Roger."

"Let's have a go now," said Snubby at once. But no one had any money on them, so they could only stand and watch. It was a very small fair—it could really hardly even be called that. There were automatic machines standing round the wall, where you could lose any amount of pennies. There was a stall to buy ice-cream and candyfloss. There was a machine that played tunes if you put money into it—loud, blaring tunes that never seemed to stop!

"A juke-box," said Snubby, airing his knowledge. He looked at the list of tunes on it. "Oh look—it can play twenty different tunes. How super! I wish they had one of these at the inn."

"Goodness—Professor James would have a blue fit!" said Diana.

"Yes—he'd go up in smoke at once," agreed Roger. "So would Mrs. Glump, I should think. Pity we haven't any money to-night."

"I don't believe Miss Pepper will let us come here much," said Diana, looking at the people who were swarming in. "They look a pretty rough lot, some of them."

A good many sailors had come in, and were climbing into the Dodgem cars with yells and whistles. One of them lurched roughly against Diana.

Roger immediately took his sister out of the place. He had been taught always to look after her, and he suddenly thought that this place wasn't right for Diana to be in at night.

"Here—where are you going, Roger?" asked Snubby in surprise. "We've only just come."

"Well, we're going," said Roger. "Come on. Let's go and see if the pierrots have begun their show."

They must have begun because a sound of very sweet singing came down the pier as the three children stood at the turnstiles. "That's Iris Nightingale," said Snubby. "I bet it is. I thought she looked sweet."

"Snubby's lost his heart to her!" said Diana. "*I* thought the Funny Man was the nicest of the three. I loved the way his ears stuck out—they were rather pointed too—like a brownie's!"

A sound of a banjo being played now came from the pier—jig-jig-jig-jiggy-jig-jig-jig! Snubby at once pretended he, too, had a banjo and began to play it earnestly, making a peculiar noise through his teeth as he did so.

"Oh stop it, Snubby," said Roger. "I suppose you think you're very funny."

"Well, I do rather," said Snubby, still going on with his banjo playing. "Everyone roars when I play my banjo at school—a pretend one, of course. I can play the zither too—listen!"

He pretended to be holding a zither, and twanged the

37

strings with much feeling, imitating the sound of a zither as he did so. He really did it very well.

A man strolling down the pier suddenly stopped and listened. He was dressed in pierrot clothes and had obviously left the show for a breath of air. He watched Snubby with amusement.

"Hey there!" he called. "Aren't you the kids at the inn? You're not bad at that fooling, youngster. Why don't you go in for our kids' competition each week—I bet you'd win it!"

Snubby stopped his imitation of a zither, and grinned at the man. "I didn't recognise you in your pierrot get-up," he said. "You're the Funny Man, aren't you?"

The man suddenly waggled his big ears, which startled the children considerably. He also made a most peculiar face which Snubby immediately longed to copy.

"Yes, I'm the Funny Man," he said. "But it isn't always funny to be funny. I get bored, you know."

He did a few ridiculous dancing steps on the pier, fell over his feet and sat down suddenly with a surprised grin. The children roared, and Loony nearly went mad trying to get off the lead and streak through the turnstiles.

"You know, we have fun in these kids' competitions," he said, getting up in one quick movement. "Anyone can go in for them. Five bob prize for the best girl, five bob for the best boy. You ought to come along and try. It doesn't matter what you do—dance, sing, conjure, play the fool. That young fellow there would win the prize for playing the fool in no time!"

He nodded at Snubby, who didn't quite know whether to take this as a compliment or not!

"Snubby's *always* playing the fool," said Roger. "It's the one thing he really works hard at. Isn't it, Snubby!"

Snubby gave Roger a punch. The man grinned and turned to go. The dance music had stopped and he was due back in his place. He threw his cigarette over the side of the pier.

"So long!" he said. "See you in the morning at the dear old inn with Ma Glump seeing that we all use our knives and forks properly, and don't speak with our mouths full."

"Makes you feel quite in the glumps, doesn't it?" said

Snubby, remembering the joke he had made before. The Funny Man laughed.

"You ought to come and be my partner," he said. "The Funny Man and the Scream of a Boy. So long!"

He went quickly up the pier. Snubby stared after him. He wasn't sure whether the man thought he, Snubby, really was funny or whether he was just making fun of him.

"Showing off!" said Roger to Snubby, in a tone of disgust. "How you can show off like that I don't know, Snubby. Come on—it's getting late. Miss Pepper will be sending out a search party soon!"

They went back to the inn. Miss Pepper met them at the door. "Roger! Diana! Who do you think has just telephoned?"

"Who?" asked everyone at once.

"Barney!" said Miss Pepper.

"BARNEY!" said all three children in delight. "Is he anywhere near then?"

"Come in and I'll tell you what he said," said Miss Pepper. She took them into the lounge which was now empty.

"I was sitting here," she said, "when Mrs. Glump came and said there was a Mr. Barnabas on the telephone for you—but would I like to go instead. I couldn't think who Mr. Barnabas was at first!

"I went, and it was Barney, of course," said Miss Pepper. "He's been ill. He sounded very lonely indeed, and I think he was longing to get in touch with the only friends he's got—you three. He gave me a telephone number and said would you ring him when you came in. It's a call box and he's waiting there now."

"Quick—we'll telephone this very minute," said Diana. "What's the number? Dear old Barney! I'd so love to see him again!"

Miss Pepper gave them the number and they rushed off to the hotel telephone. Barney! How lovely! If only he was somewhere near and could come to Rubadub.

Barney was their circus-boy friend. They had met him by accident, with Miranda, his clever little monkey—and had been firm friends ever since. He was all alone in the world, and kept himself by taking jobs in circuses and

39

fairs. Now he had been ill—he was lonely. The three children longed to ask him all his news.

Roger and the others crowded into the little telephone box. Roger rang the number. Barney's voice answered at once. "Hallo! Is that you, Roger?"

"Hallo, Barney! Where are you? I hear you've been ill. Are you all right again? How's Miranda?"

"She's fine," said Barney. "I got a chill or something—sleeping under a hedge in the rain. I had to lie up in a barn for a week or two—and Miranda looked after me!"

"Good old Miranda!" said Roger, having a mental vision of the little monkey sponging Barney's face, and bringing him cups of water to drink! "Where are you, Barney? How did you know we were here?"

"I telephoned your home," said Barney. "Your cook told me. Listen—I can get a lift almost to your place to-morrow. Just a stroke of luck. I've been a bit lonely lately —that chill, I suppose."

It was so unlike Barney to admit that he felt lonely that Roger knew at once he must be feeling very miserable. He remembered how he had felt when he had the 'flu in the spring—and he had been surrounded by people eager to help and comfort him. Barney had had nobody but Miranda!

"You come down here," urged Roger at once. "Come and stay at our inn. Oh, wait though—I'm sure Mrs. Glump wouldn't have Miranda. Blow!"

"I can't possibly come and stay where you are," said Barney at once. "For one thing, I've no money and for another, they wouldn't have me there. But I can find some kind of a job, I'm sure, and I can always sleep on the beach in this fine weather. I'd like that."

"All right. Anyway—COME," said Roger. "We'll be on the look-out for you. Oh, Barney, how super to have you here! Give our love to darling Miranda! Loony will be thrilled to see her."

"I'll come," said Barney. "Good-bye, Roger." There was a click in Roger's ear as the telephone receiver was put down at Barney's end. Roger put his down too. The others immediately plied him with questions.

Roger squeezed out of the box with the other two pressing on him, so eager to hear what he had to say that they couldn't wait to get out of the box properly.

They all went into the lounge, where Miss Pepper was waiting for them. Roger told them word for word what Barney had said.

"So he'll be here in Rubadub to-morrow," he said exultantly. "Good old Barney! It will be grand to see him again, and Miranda too."

"Smashing," said Snubby, who was very fond of the sturdy, self-reliant Barney, and his amusing mischievous little monkey.

"Now go to bed, please," said Miss Pepper, who was longing to go herself. "And please *do* be down in time for breakfast!"

CHAPTER EIGHT

DEAR OLD BARNEY

THE CHILDREN slept so soundly that they didn't even hear the loud breakfast gong. Miss Pepper came bustling into their rooms just after it went, only half-dressed, with her dressing-gown still on!

"Wake up, do!" she said. "I've overslept as well. Dear me, we shall make a very bad impression on Mrs. Glump if we are so late the first morning. Can you be very quick?"

"No," said Snubby sleepily, and turned over.

"Barney may be here at any time," said Miss Pepper artfully.

Snubby shot out of bed at once. "I'd forgotten old Barney," he said. Miss Pepper left the boys dressing quickly, made sure that Diana was also getting up, and went to finish her own dressing. They were so late that only Miss Twitt was in the lounge!

She greeted them beamingly. "You poor things! Did you oversleep? The dear children must have been so tired —and the dear dog too!"

The dear dog was not in the least tired. He trotted up to Miss Twitt, removed her napkin from her knee and made off with it. It was a silly trick he had picked up, most annoying to everyone. Miss Twitt gave a little squeal.

"Oh, naughty, naughty! Bring it back then."

"LOONY!" roared Snubby, in his most stentorian voice. "BRING IT HERE!"

Miss Twitt almost fell out of her chair at this roar, and the noise brought the contemptuous-looking Mr. Tubby to the door. He gazed in inquiringly, looking more miserable than ever, with his baggy wrinkles falling over his doggy face. Loony backed away from him and dropped the napkin. Mr. Tubby sniffed at it, picked it up and took it to his rug. He lay down heavily on it, creaking and groaning.

"There, Loony! He'll take *you* next and drop you on his rug and lie down on you," threatened Snubby, hoping that he wouldn't have to go and rescue Miss Twitt's napkin from the formidable Mr. Tubby.

"Dear Mr. Tubby," gushed Miss Twitt. "Isn't he a *remarkable* dog? I do love dogs, don't you, Miss Pepper. I love cats, too, the dear dainty things!"

"You'd like our cat Sardine then, Miss Twitter," began Snubby. "She likes to trip people up on the stairs in a very dainty way. Oh, and Miss Twitter, you'd love a monkey that belongs to a friend of ours."

"Yes, dear, I'm sure I should," said Miss Twitt. "But my name is Twitt, not Twitter."

"I just *can't* remember," said Snubby, deliberately not looking towards Miss Pepper, who was wearing a fierce and warning frown. "It reminds me of a song I know—twit-twit-twitter little bird—something like that anyway. I do so *love* birds, don't you, Miss Twitter. I think they're sweet."

"Snubby, will you go and get me a handkerchief, please," said Miss Pepper desperately. How could she stop this awful chatter of Snubby's? It was sending Diana into helpless giggles, and Roger was grinning from ear to ear. Even Miss Pepper, angry as she was, couldn't help thinking that Miss Twitt deserved to have fun poked at her—how very, very silly she was! Twittering away like that.

Snubby gave a surprised glance at Miss Pepper. "'Tisn't often you forget *your* handkerchief," he remarked. He caught her eye and decided to say no more. He went meekly off and returned with a handkerchief. Miss Twitt beamed and looked as if she was about to make a remark about helpful little boys, Miss Pepper charged in desperately before she could say a word.

"I wonder when Barney will arrive, Roger. Did he say any time? We must look out for him."

This was such an interesting theme of conversation that all three immediately forgot about Miss Twitt, and she soon left her table and went out of the room with a swish of skirts, a rattle of bracelets and a sudden waft of rather strong perfume.

"Pooh!" said Snubby. "What's that awful smell?"

Miss Pepper took the opportunity of explaining very clearly and concisely to Snubby exactly what she thought of discourtesy and impoliteness, and threatened such dreadful things that Snubby sank back in his chair, amazed.

"I say!" he said feebly. "I'm sorry. She kind of sets me off, you know, with her twittering. She's too good to be true. Miss Pepper, you don't really mean to say you'd make me go without cake for a whole week, and only let me have one helping of anything? You couldn't be so cruel."

"I could and I shall," said Miss Pepper severely. "I will not have rudeness even if you mean it to be funny rudeness. Now, finish up that toast and marmalade for goodness' sake. I don't want to sit here till dinner-time."

They all bathed that morning. The water was warm, and although there was little wind, there were very satisfactory waves some way out to dive through.

"I like to cut through a wave just as it's breaking," said Diana. "It spills its green colour all over me. I say—it's going to be super here, isn't it?"

They kept a look-out for Barney and Miranda, but they didn't appear that morning. They all went on the beach in the afternoon to read and laze. The sun shone down on them and they began to turn a lobster red. They were all in swim-suits and Miss Pepper thought they would feel very uncomfortable if they got much more burnt!

"Loony wishes he could take off his coat and wear a swim-suit too," said Diana, patting the panting dog. "Hasn't he got a long tongue when he hangs it out? Do you want an ice-cream, Loony?"

"Woof," said Loony at once, scrambling up. "Ice-cream" was one of the words he understood very well! But as everyone was too lazy to go and buy any, Loony lay down again mournfully. Fancy raising his hopes for nothing! He began to pant heavily once more, making Diana feel hotter than ever.

One by one they fell asleep in the sand. Diana lay on her back, her sun-hat fitted over her face. Roger lay on his side, curled up comfortably. Snubby lay on his tummy, and his back got redder and redder. Miss Pepper slept in a dignified manner in a deck-chair, with a sunshade over her head.

Somebody came scampering over the sands. Somebody leapt right in the middle of Snubby's back and jumped up and down there, chattering. Loony gave an enormous bark and planted his front paws on Snubby's back too.

Miss Pepper woke up with a jump. Snubby woke too and yelled angrily, "Get off, idiot! Who's that banging my back? Get off, I tell you, it's sore!"

He rolled over and somebody suddenly cuddled into his neck, making a little chattering noise of welcome.

44

"MIRANDA!" yelled Snubby. "Oh, Miranda, it's you! Hey, look, Miranda's here. Where's Barney?"

The whole group then became extremely wide awake and lively. Loony went mad, of course, and raced round and round them, kicking up sand as he went. Miranda leapt from one to another, chattering and hugging and snuggling.

Snubby stood up and looked along the promenade. He saw a figure he recognised at once. "Barney! Barney, here we are! Come on, Barney!"

By this time every one on the beach was aware that a boy with a monkey had arrived, and was being loudly welcomed by his friends! Barney jumped down from the promenade and made his way over the sand, grinning. Diana flew to meet him.

"Barney! You've come! Oh, Barney, you've gone thin!"

Barney sat down with his friends, his face beaming. His strange, wide-set eyes were as brilliantly blue as ever and his corn-coloured hair was the same thick mop. His wide mouth smiled happily as he looked from one to another of his friends.

"It's grand to see you," he said. "It seems ages since May when we were at Ring O' Bells together. And now we're at Rubadub-on-Sea! You're looking fine, all of you."

"You've been ill, poor Barney," said Diana. "You look thin and you're not as brown as usual."

"Oh, I'm better now," said Barney. "Miranda looked after me, as I told you. I got a chill, I think—sleeping in the rain. I lay in a barn and coughed for days. The farmer let me be there, and Miranda fetched and carried for me! She went to the farmhouse each day and brought back the bread and stuff the farmer gave her. You should have seen her carrying mugs of milk too—never spilt a drop, did you, Miranda?"

Diana's eyes suddenly filled with tears. She could see Barney lying alone and ill with only a little monkey to see to him. How *awful* to be alone as that—no mother, no father, no friends to rally round! Dear little Miranda— how worried and puzzled she must have been!

"You must have been awfully lonely," said Snubby who, because he had no parents, understood a little more than the others what it meant to be on his own—though Snubby had plenty of kind relations!

"Yes. I'm not usually lonely," said Barney. "I wished my mother wasn't dead. And I wished I could find my father. Just imagine having a father alive somewhere, and you don't know who he is or where he is! He doesn't know anything about me, I know—but all the same we belong, don't we?"

Miss Pepper was listening. She knew all about Barney's history, of course—how his mother, a circus-girl had married an actor, and had run away from him after three months to go back to the life she loved, in the circus. Barney had been born six months later, but she hadn't bothered to let his father know, afraid that he might want to have Barney for himself.

So Barney had grown up thinking that his father was dead—and it was only when his mother was ill that she had told him her secret—how she had run away from his father, and had never even told him about his son! But no doubt his father was alive, and Barney must look for him, she had said.

And Barney *had* looked for him, but had never found him. What was he like? Was he still an actor? He had acted in Shakespeare's plays, that was all Barney knew. If only he could find the one person who really belonged to him!

"We'll find your father for you," said Diana, unable to bear the loneliness in Barney's voice. "We will, we will! *SOMEHOW* there must be a way, Barney!"

CHAPTER NINE

LAZY AFTERNOON

BARNEY FELT better at once when he had told his troubles and fears and longings to his three friends. He had brooded over them after his illness and hadn't been able to get them out of his mind.

"But now you've told us all about everything, and we'll all do our best to get things right for you, you'll feel different, won't you?" said Diana anxiously. She could never bear people to be miserable.

"I feel different already," said Barney, half ashamed of telling his troubles. "I shall feel a mutt to-night when I think of all I've told you."

"Well, what's the good of having friends if you don't share your troubles?" said Roger sensibly. "It simply means you trust us."

"Yes. It means that all right," said Barney. "But *you* don't share your troubles with me—you never seem to have any. Perhaps people don't when they've got families to belong to."

"Oh yes they do," said Snubby feelingly. "You wait till you get into trouble with Uncle Richard like I do—and get one of his whackings. That's trouble all right. Unfortunately I can't ask anyone to share it."

"Don't forget that friends share their good things as well as their troubles," said Miss Pepper. "Seeing we're all friends together, what about sharing our tea, and a few ice-creams?"

"Golly—is it teatime already?" said Snubby, sitting up hurriedly. "Fancy—I was so pleased at seeing old Barney, I actually forgot all about tea!"

"What a wonderful compliment to Barney," said Diana, stroking Miranda, who was surely the happiest little monkey in the world at that moment. "I shouldn't think anything or anybody made you forget about a meal before."

Barney laughed. This was the sort of silly family talk he loved and never had unless he was with his three friends. All that answering back and idiotic jokes and teasing—it was lovely to him, though Miss Pepper, of course, often got tired of it.

The children had brought tea down to the beach. Mrs. Glump had graciously said that she would have it packed up for them, and had supplied a quite enormous number of sandwiches, buns, slices of fruit cake and some home-made shortbread biscuits that really melted in their mouths.

"This is some tea!" said Snubby, with much appreciation. "I wouldn't have thought Mrs. Glump would have given us such a spread. But she's not as glumpish as she looks."

"She probably hoped that by giving you far too much to

eat at teatime, you would eat less at dinner," remarked Miss Pepper, with amusement.

"What a hope!" said Snubby. "It doesn't make the slightest difference as far as I am concerned. You know I always feel frightfully sorry for you grown-ups, Miss Pepper. It must be awful never to have a really good tuck-in because you feel it might be rude or greedy."

"You'll hate being grown-up, won't you, Snubby?" said Diana. "No big meals. No half-dozen ice-creams one after the other. No munching of chocolate bars half the day. No . . ."

"Don't," said Snubby in alarm. "Come on, Barney, have another sandwich."

But Barney's appetite was not what it once had been. Miss Pepper thought he must indeed have been very ill. She wondered what he was going to do now. She wished she could have him at the inn and feed him and look after him a bit. But that was impossible. Nobody there would think of having Miranda, for one thing, and Barney would certainly not be parted from her.

Also, he was rather down-at-heel and untidy. He had done his best to look clean and neat for his friends, but he had had no money for some time, and it was impossible even to buy new sandshoes. So he wore none, and his feet were brown and bare. His shirt was torn and had no buttons, and his grey flannel trousers were patched about the knees and frayed at the ends.

But what a fine boy he was—good-looking, trustworthy, intelligent and straightforward. A boy any father could be proud of. Miss Pepper looked at Barney and sighed. She felt sure that Barney would never find his father, but she hadn't the heart to say so.

"Barney, I *wish* you could come and stay at the inn with us," said Diana.

"I couldn't," said Barney. You know that. Anyway, I've got myself a job."

They all stared at him in admiration. A job already! How *did* he do it!

"What job?" asked Roger.

"Well, there's a kind of a small fair in the town," began Barney. "With Dodgem cars and things."

"Oh yes! We went there last night!" cried Diana. "Have you got a job there, Barney?"

"Yes. I'm good at machinery, you know," said Barney. "I'm in charge of the cars—got to keep the machinery oiled and all the cars in running order and so on. It's an easy job for me. I like fairs, too—it's my life and always has been, going about with fairs and circuses!"

"Well, you'll be able to be with us quite a lot, won't you?" said Snubby eagerly. "This fair isn't open till after tea."

"Yes, I guess I can be with you quite a bit," said Barney, pleased. "I won't come to the inn, though. They'd look down their noses at me—I don't look very ship-shape at the moment. But when I've got a bit of money I'll soon spruce myself up."

All the three wanted immediately to offer Barney every penny they had, either as a gift or as a loan—but they said nothing. Barney was surprisingly proud. It made him feel ashamed and embarrassed if they offered too much.

However, Miss Pepper had an offer to make and she made it briskly.

"There's one thing you can certainly do, Barney. Borrow a swim-suit from Roger—and while you're bathing I can sew buttons on your shirt and mend the frayed ends of your trousers. They look quite clean, so I shan't need to wash them."

"Well—thanks," said Barney, flushing. "I'm not too good at doing things like that."

Roger rushed off and fetched a swim-suit from the inn. Barney went behind a rock and came out again almost immediately in Roger's bathing trunks. He handed his shirt and trousers shyly to Miss Pepper.

"Thanks a lot," he said. "You're really kind. Gosh, it's wonderful to be back with you all again. Loony too—mad old Loony!"

Loony's cup of joy was full and running over now that he had Barney and Miranda as well as everyone else. He raced round the beach at top speed, barked as he passed the others, dodged round Miranda, barked in her ear, and then went off again at sixty miles an hour.

"Express train act," said Snubby. "He'll probably be tired out in a minute and come and flop down beside Miranda—and she'll play a few of her tricks on him."

It happened exactly as Snubby had said. Loony, quite exhausted, and panting like a train going uphill, flung herself down on the sand by the others. Miranda leapt on to his back and pulled up his big, floppy ears. Up he got and tried to shake her off, but she hung on, chattering excitedly.

Loony tore off with her, hoping to jerk her off, much to the amusement of everyone else on the beach. But Miranda stuck on, enjoying her ride immensely, bumping up and down on Loony's back as if he were a little black race-horse!

He suddenly remembered how to get rid of the annoying little monkey! He rolled over on his back and Miranda promptly sprang off, afraid of being rolled on. She scampered back to Barney and leapt into his arms before Loony could catch her.

A man came slowly up to them—a tall, thin man whom the children recognised at once. It was the conjurer belonging to the pierrot show. He had watched Miranda and Barney and an idea had suddenly struck him. He saw that Barney was dressed poorly and guessed that he had to work for his living.

"You boy," he said, when he came up, pointing to Barney.

"Do you want a job? I'm a magician—a conjurer with the pierrot show on the pier. If you like to come there with your monkey as my assistant, I'll give you good wages. What about it, son?"

"Sorry, sir. But I've just got a job," said Barney. "Down with the Dodgem cars. But it if doesn't turn out well, I'll come and tell you. I've got to stay there a week though."

The conjurer nodded and walked away. Barney turned to the others. "Did you see his eyes?" he said. "I bet he's a queer fellow. I guess I wouldn't like to work with those piercing eyes on me! They'd send shivers down my spine. He's the kind of fellow who can see out of the back of his head!"

"All the same, I think it's marvellous to be offered a job just like that!" said Snubby enviously. "I bet nobody would ever offer *me* a job out of the air. I bet it would take me months to find one."

It was a lovely lazy afternoon. Miss Pepper went for a walk about six o'clock and left the little company alone. They told Barney all about the guests at the hotel, especially Miss Twitter. They told him about the funny little hall-porter, Dummy. Barney looked up at once.

"Dummy? What's he like? Tell me."

They described him. "Little—with a big head and round blue eyes—a button of a mouth—and frightfully strong," said Roger. "He's not properly grown-up, I think—sort of half-child, half-adult. I like him. The taxi-driver told us he got into awful rages at times. Why—have you ever met him?"

"Well, it *must* be the Dummy I once knew," said Barney. "He was in a circus with me some years ago. He was always very fond of my mother, who was kind to him. I left that circus and never knew what became of him. Dear old Dummy! I liked him—he was really just a kind-hearted child—but he certainly could get into savage tempers. He was dangerous then, with his extraordinary strength. I've seen him pick up a man and throw him into the air!"

"Goodness!" said Roger, startled at this new light on Dummy. "Well, you'll have to go and see if it's the Dummy you know. We'll tell him about you."

Miss Pepper came back and called them. "Dinner time," she said. It was the one call that always made them hurry! "Good-bye, Barney, see you to-morrow!" Snubby yelled. "Look after yourself!"

CHAPTER TEN

A WORD WITH DUMMY

MISS PEPPER wouldn't let the children go down to the little fair after dinner. "No," she said. "It will be Barney's first night. He ought to have nothing to attend to but his job."

"We shan't disturb him!" said Snubby indignantly. But Roger saw Miss Pepper's point. It wouldn't be fair on Barney when he was busy learning a new job to have three friends, to say nothing of Loony, trying to get his attention, or embarrassing him by watching him at work.

They decided to go and find Dummy and see if he knew Barney. Mrs. Glump was surprised when they asked if they might talk to Dummy.

"We think we've met a friend of his," explained Roger. "We just want to talk to him and find out."

"But you won't get anything out of poor old Dummy," said Mrs. Glump. "He hardly ever says a word. He can imitate noises. Boom-boom—bang-bang—ch-ch-ch, like a train—mew-mew like a cat. But he doesn't talk."

"Could we see him, all the same, though?" asked Roger.

"He'll be out in the back-yard," said Mrs. Glump, not very graciously. They went to the back of the dark hall, pushed open a baize-covered door, and went into a great kitchen. A door led out from there into the back-yard. It was a horrid little place, full of piled-up rubbish of all kinds, empty bottles, crates, boxes, old decaying vegetables, and a large tabby cat.

The cat immediately vaulted up to high wall when Loony appeared. Loony, of course, felt sure he could jump the wall and began to fling himself at it madly.

Dummy was there, sweeping up the rubbish when Loony rushed into the yard, Dummy turned round and saw the children, and his face became just like an amiable child's.

"Woof-woof" he said, pointing to Loony.

"Hallo, Dummy," said Snubby. "We want to ask you something."

Dummy's face clouded over. He obviously didn't like being asked questions. They confused his mind. He didn't mind being told to do things—but he couldn't bear to be asked anything. That meant he had to think of an answer.

"It's all right, Dummy," said Diana, noticing his frown. "We just want to tell you something. We met a friend of ours to-day who thinks he once knew you. A boy called Barney."

Dummy thought hard and then shook his head. The children were disappointed.

"It can't have been the Dummy that Barney knew," said Roger. "And yet—Barney said he was exactly like our description of *this* Dummy!"

Diana suddenly had an idea. She turned back to Dummy, who was regarding the three children anxiously.

"Dummy," said Diana, "Barney had a monkey—a dear little monkey called Miranda. Do you remember *her*?"

A brilliant smile transformed Dummy's anxious face. He threw down his broom and clasped his arms together, rocking them as if he were holding some small creature.

"Monkey!" he said at last. And then with a great effort he brought out the word "Barney." He nodded his head up and down violently, swept with sudden memories. "Barney, Barney, Barney," he said. He pulled at Diana's arm. He pointed round and about as if asking where Barney was.

"He's got a job down at the little fair—where the Dodgem cars are, you know," said Diana.

"Is good, good, good," said Dummy in a transport of delight. Then he caught sight of Mrs. Glump at one of the windows and snatched up his broom again. He began to sweep wildly, sending the rubbish here, there and everywhere.

"Come on—we'd better go. We've excited him so much that he won't be able to sweep anything up properly if we don't go away," said Roger. "I wonder what time he goes off duty. I bet he'll go straight down to the fair to find Barney."

"I do like Dummy," said Diana. "I'm sure he'd be able to talk all right if people were kind to him."

"I'm going to be very nice to him to make up for all the people who probably haven't," announced Snubby, rather fiercely. "I like him too. He reminds me a bit of Loony—sort of faithful and loyal and all that."

"He's not a *bit* like Loony," said Diana. "Loony's crazy! Look at him now, still thinking he can jump over that wall. Loony, come here. That cat is laughing at you."

They disappeared through the kitchen door, and came out in the hall. It was dark there. They debated what to do.

"Let's see if there's anyone in the lounge," said Snubby "If it's empty we might go in and play cards. But if Miss Twitter's there I shall run for miles!"

Miss Twitter wasn't there. But Professor James was. Fortunately, however, he was fast asleep in the big armchair. "We could bring our cards here and just play a *quiet* game for half an hour," said Diana. "He's asleep—and besides he's deaf. He probably won't hear a single sound."

Roger fetched the cards. They sat down round a little table to play, and Roger dealt out the cards. He glanced round at the old Professor to see if he was soundly asleep. If he still was, they could talk in normal voices.

They played two games and then gathered up the cards, wondering if there was time for more. Snubby remembered the little stairway up to the roof, where a view could be got of the sea on the other side of the cliff.

"I wish we could get out of that skylight, walk across the roof to the cliff, and then sit down in that cleft to see the Secret Submarine Base," he said. "We might spot something quite interesting."

"We shouldn't," said Roger. "It's too far away. It's a funny little staircase, isn't it? I wonder what it was first used for—I mean—it doesn't seem to serve any useful purpose."

"There used to be smugglers here in the old days," said Snubby. "Miss Pepper told me. I wouldn't be surprised if that old staircase up to that roof had some use then—you know—signalling that a smuggling ship had come in."

"Or it might have been used by wreckers," said Diana. "The men who used to send ships on to rocks by wrong signals, so that they could make money out of the wreck."

"Horrible creatures!" said Snubby. "I can't understand people like that."

"You might have done it yourself if you'd lived in those days," said Diana.

"I would not," said Snubby, raising his voice. "How can you say such a thing?"

Roger was listening idly, flipping the cards in his hands. He happened to glance into a mirror opposite him, which clearly reflected the old Professor, who was in a chair a little way behind him.

Had he got his eyes open? It looked exactly as if he had! It looked as if he were wide awake—and yet he hadn't said a word to stop them playing or talking! Roger turned quickly—but no, the old man's eyes were fast shut.

Roger was puzzled. Had he been mistaken? It really had looked as if the reflection showed the old man with his eyes open—why should he pretend to be asleep?

The other two were still arguing. Snubby was angry—how could Diana think he would ever be a wrecker?

"Don't shout," said Diana. "You'll waken the old man."

"I don't care," said Snubby rudely. "I just wish Loony

would jump on him and give him a fright. It's awful for a dog to have to lie as still as a mouse under a table!"

Roger looked into the mirror again. There—he was *sure* the old man had his eyes open again! He was looking at Roger's back, listening to what was being said about him.

Roger turned round quickly—but again the old man's eyes were closed. When Roger turned round to the mirror the eyes were closed there too. He was puzzled. Why was he pretending to be asleep? Just to listen while they went on talking? But then, he was deaf, wasn't he? What was the point then.

Roger gave it up. If an old gentleman liked to pretend he was deaf and asleep, and listen like a sneak to what others were saying, then he could get on with it.

He suddenly determined to find out for certain if the old man was deaf—and asleep. He leaned across the table, and winked at the others. They knew something was up, and looked at him expectantly.

"Listen," said Roger in a sinister sort of voice. "There's no one about except that old fellow there, who is deaf and fast asleep. We can have a few words about What We Know."

"Aha, yes," said Snubby, wondering what was up but quite prepared to fall in with any silly game of Roger's. "About the Man Who Whispers, you mean. And the one with the False Passport."

"That's it," hissed Roger. "Once we find out their Password, we can get going. We must look out for a man in disguise."

"Yes. But can you tell him by one of his little fingers—it's crooked," said Snubby, remembering one of the naval men he had seen on the train and putting him into his silly story.

Diana stared open-mouthed at the two boys. What in the world was all this? Had they gone mad?

Roger looked hurriedly into the mirror. The old man's eyes were wide open. He was certainly listening now. Well, much good it would do him! If he began believing all they said it would give him a lot to think about!

A voice came in at the door, making them all jump violently. It was Miss Pepper.

"Haven't you gone upstairs *yet*! Oh dear—is that the

Professor there? I didn't see him at first or I wouldn't have spoken so loudly.

"It's all right," said Roger, getting up. "He's fast asleep!"

CHAPTER ELEVEN

MORE ABOUT BARNEY

NEXT DAY was rather exciting. For one thing, Barney had discovered that Dummy *was* the old friend he had once known. He was very pleased about it.

They all met down on the beach in the morning. Miranda was excited and talkative. She began to dig herself a little hole to sit in, imitating the children. Loony watched her, his tongue hanging out. Miranda suddenly reached up a quick paw and pulled it hard. Loony yelped.

"Well, keep your tongue in then, Loony," said Snubby. "It's just an invitation to Miranda if you stand over her, hanging it out half-way down your chest. You're a very silly dog to let a monkey get the better of you."

Loony wandered away, offended. Barney began to tell them about Dummy. "I was just finishing my work at the fair last night," he said, "when my boss said 'Chap to see you, Barney.' And in walked old Dummy!"

"Was he pleased to see you?" asked Diana.

"Pleased! I should think so. He took both my hands in his and worked them up and down as if they were a pump handle!" said Barney. "Then Miranda spotted him and she knew him at once. Miranda never forgets anyone, you know. She took a flying leap on to his shoulder, and he cradled her in his arms just like he did when she was a tiny little thing. He crooned to her like he always used to. I nearly howled!"

"Did he talk to you at all?" asked Roger. "He doesn't seem able to talk very much."

"Well, he's not British, to begin with," said Barney, "and he never was much good at picking up our language. But he can talk when he wants to, if he's happy and people are friendly. He couldn't say a word to me at first but he said plenty later on, when he came back to my lodgings with me."

"What did you talk about?" asked Diana curiously. "Your old friends?"

"Yes. And my mother," said Barney. He paused. "Dummy didn't know she had died. He cried when I told him, because he was very fond of her. She was so kind to him. But he said I'd grown quite unlike her."

"How?" asked Roger.

"Well—she was dark and I'm fair. She had brown eyes and I've got blue. She was little and I'm tall. I am sorry I wasn't like her."

"You must be like your father then," said Diana, looking at Barney's strange blue eyes. "That will make it easier when we try to find him. We'll look for someone just like you!"

"I wish I *could* find him," said Barney. "A father's no end of a help when you're growing up. Of course—I might not like him. He might not like me either. He might even be ashamed of me."

"Why did your mother run away from him?" asked Diana. "Was he unkind to her?"

"I don't know. I guess she couldn't live in a house after she'd lived in a caravan all her life," said Barney. "I guess she hankered after the life she knew. But I wish she'd sent word to my father when I was born. It's awful to think he doesn't know about me. He might not believe my story, if ever I do find him."

"What's your surname, Barney?" asked Roger, suddenly realising that they didn't know.

"Lorimer," said Barney. "My full name is Barnabas Hugo Lorimer—what a mouthful! But Lorimer isn't my father's name—it's my mother's. She used her own name again when she ran away, and I never even knew it wasn't my rightful surname till just before she died. She didn't tell me my real name—I don't think she thought to tell me, and I never thought of asking her, because I somehow thought Lorimer was her married name, you see. I never realised it would be important."

"What about your birth certificate?" asked Diana, remembering hers. "That would have everything on it, wouldn't it?"

"What's a birth certificate?" asked Barney, looking startled. "I never heard of one before. Anyway, I haven't got one, whatever it is."

There was a silence. The three children were all thinking the same thing. How hopeless to try and find a man when you didn't know in the least what he was like, or how old he was, or even what his name was! Why, he might be staying in the same town and none of them would know!

Roger made up his mind to ask Miss Pepper's help. She would know how to set about things. Anyway, they did know that Barney's father acted—or used to act, in Shakespeare's plays. That was something.

Loony appeared, carrying some article in his mouth. "Now what's he got?" said Snubby. "Loony, if you bring that dead crab again I'll make you eat it. It was a bad enough crab yesterday and to-day it'll be worse."

It wasn't a crab. It was a man's hair-brush! Snubby took it out of Loony's mouth and glared at him. "Bad dog! Didn't I tell you when you come to stay at an inn or hotel you don't pinch people's brushes? You're not at home. Whose brush is this, I'd like to know!"

"Woof," said Loony, pleased with himself.

"Do you mean to say you've been all the way back to

the inn, popped upstairs, found an open door and grabbed a brush?" said Snubby. "You must be mad!"

"He's just showing off," said Diana. "He's trying to show Miranda something she can't do."

"Don't say that!" said Barney quickly. "You know how she imitates every one. I don't want *her* arriving with brushes. I should get into awful trouble."

"So will Loony," said Snubby severely. He smacked the surprised spaniel on his nose with the brush. "Why have you always had this passion for brushes? You are *not* to take brushes, towels *or* mats away, Loony!"

Loony backed hurriedly away from another smack and sat down on Miranda. He got up again just as hurriedly, feeling sharp teeth in his tail. He yelped and leaped on to Snubby.

"Don't play musical chairs with me and Miranda," said Snubby, pushing him off. "I'm still cross with you." He examined the brush. It had the initials M.M. on it in silver.

"Matthew Marvel," said Diana tracing them with her finger. "He's the conjurer. His bedroom is on the same landing as ours. Loony must have found his door a bit ajar, pushed it, and gone in. I believe he thinks that all the rooms there are his to wander round. I found him in there yesterday."

"Well, I'll return it to dear Matthew some time to-day," said Snubby. "I don't feel I can go back this very minute. Let's bathe!"

So they bathed, Miranda wouldn't go into the water, but danced up and down at the edge of the waves, holding up her little red skirt, much to the amusement of all the children nearby. Loony leapt into the water boldly, trying to keep up with Snubby. Barney swam the best. He was already feeling much better, partly because he was happy again. He thought warmly of his three friends—no, four, counting Loony. Whatever happened, he would never, never lose them.

"Can you come out with us this afternoon, Barney?" asked Roger, as they lay drying in the sun after their bathe.

"Oh yes. I'm not on duty till half-past five," said Barney. "What are you doing?"

"We haven't thought," said Snubby. "I'd like to take a boat out, I think."

"Yes. Good idea," said Roger. "I say—let's row out to Rubadub Whirlpool—I'd love to see that."

"What's that?" asked Barney, interested.

They all told him at once. "It's not very far out—it's towards the cliff that separates our little bay from the Submarine Bay," said Snubby, when Barney had disentangled all the descriptions of the whirlpool.

"Right. We'll get a boat and go there this afternoon," said Barney. "I'd like to see that. I've never seen a proper whirlpool before."

It was lunch-time, so they parted and Roger and the others hurried back to the inn—not because they were late, of course, but because they were overcome with hunger! They ran upstairs to wash and tidy themselves.

"I'd better return Mr. Marvel's brush," said Snubby. "I hope he's not in. If he isn't I could steal into his room and put it back. Then I shouldn't have to explain Loony's idiotic behaviour!"

Snubby knocked quietly. He listened. There was no sound from inside at all. He turned the handle of the door quietly and slid in without a sound, the brush in his hand.

He stopped suddenly. Mr. Marvel was there after all. He sat at a table strewn with cards on which were many numbers of all kinds. He was studying them, and then writing rapidly. Snubby didn't quite know what to do. He gave a polite little cough.

Mr. Marvel leapt to his feet immediately and turned a furious face on Snubby, covering up the cards with his hand. "What is it, what do you want, how dare you sneak in like this?" he demanded in a harsh voice. Then he realised that it was only Snubby, and forced a smile on his long, lean face.

"You silly boy—you startled me! I was just working out one of my conjuring tricks—lost in thought—deep in meditation—and you gave me such a start. What is it you want?"

"I'm sorry to say, sir, that my dog took your brush out of your room some time this morning," said Snubby, still feeling a little scared of the furious face he had just seen. "I've brought it back."

"Oh, thanks," said the conjurer, and took it. He put it down and pulled Snubby to him. "Why don't you wash your ears, boy?" he said.

"I do," said Snubby indignantly.

"Well, well—you've got potatoes growing behind each one," said the conjurer, and removed two small potatoes from behind Snubby's ears. Snubby stared, open-mouthed.

"And why keep watches in your mouth?" said Mr. Marvel, with a little laugh. "Anyone can see them then and take them—like this!" And he inserted finger and thumb into Snubby's mouth and brought out two small watches.

"I say—look, I say," began Snubby, amazed.

"And whatever is that bulging out your shorts' pockets?" asked the conjurer. Snubby looked down, astonished. His pockets were bulging out untidly! He put in his hands and pulled out two carrots from one and an apple from the other. He held them, staring in amazement.

"Food for a little donkey," said Mr. Marvel, and laughed softly. "You do like carrots, don't you? Have them with your dinner!"

CHAPTER TWELVE

RUBADUB WHIRLPOOL

THE OTHERS had gone down to lunch. They couldn't wait for Snubby. Nor could Loony, who was also feeling decidedly ravenous. Miss Pepper looked coldly at Snubby.

"You've been a long time," she said. "What happened to you?"

"Oh, nothing much," said Snubby airily. "Mr. Marvel found some potatoes in my ears, and two watches in my mouth and some fruit and vegetables in my pockets, that's all!"

"Do you mean he did some magic tricks on you?" asked Diana. "You lucky thing! But I don't believe he took any watches out of your mouth."

"Well, I *wondered* what that ticking noise was that I heard this morning," said Roger. "Gosh, Snubby, you might have let *me* take them out of your mouth."

"He was pretty furious when he suddenly turned round and saw me standing there," said Snubby. "He shot out of his chair, and covered up some cards with his hand as if I'd come to sneak in on his magic. He said I'd disturbed him working out a magic trick. I can't make out if I like him or not."

Mr. Marvel came into the room at that moment, and Miss Pepper signed to Snubby to change the subject. The Funny Man also came in, with Iris Nightingale in a very pretty blue and white frock that took Snubby's eye at once. He grinned at her and she smiled back.

"She's *aw*fully nice!" he said. "I had a word with her this morning. She says we really must go to the show and she'll sing me my favourite songs."

"Well, I only hope she knows 'Ride a Cock-horse to Banbury Cross' and 'Where did you come from, Baby dear?'" said Roger solemnly and rather loudly.

"Shut up. She'll hear," said Snubby fiercely. "You want a bang on the head, Roger."

"Snubby, behave yourself," said Miss Pepper, much to his indignation. He sat back, sulking, scowling at Miss Pepper. A bird flew in at the open window and fluttered round the room and then flew out. Snubby saw a way of annoying Miss Pepper, and paying her out for insulting him in public.

"Oh, did you see that dear little dicky-bird?" he said, turning round to Miss Twitt with a sweet smile. "I'm sure it twittered. I do so *love* birds, don't you, Miss Twitter."

For once in a way Miss Twitt looked at him coldly. "It's funny your little boy has such a bad memory for names, isn't it, Miss Pepper?" she said. "But there—not all of us can have brains, can we?"

"One in the eye for you, Snubby," said Roger in a low voice. The Funny Man had heard all this and he gave a guffaw which exasperated Snubby. At all costs he must change the subject. "Miss Pepper, we're going to get a boat and row to Rubadub Whirlpool this afternoon," he said loudly.

"Then you must go with a boatman," said Miss Pepper at once. The three children stared in dismay.

"Oh *why*?" asked Roger. "You *know* we can manage a boat by ourselves perfectly well."

"I don't know anything of the sort," said Miss Pepper. "And anyway you are *not* visiting whirlpools by yourselves."

"Quite right," said an unexpected voice. "A most dangerous place. Far better for children to keep away from it!"

It was Mr. Marvel speaking. Professor James put his hand behind his ear and spoke loudly.

"What's that? What's that you're talking about?"

"RUBADUB WHIRLPOOL!" shouted Snubby, and made everyone jump.

"Ah, very dangerous place," agreed the Professor. "Shouldn't let them go, Mam."

"Nor should I," said Miss Twitt, shuddering. "Whirlpools suck people down, don't they—and boats too. Down, down, down—it's terrible to think of."

"But, Miss Pepper—there are big advertisements all over the place saying it's just an afternoon trip in a boat," protested Snubby angrily. "We won't go alone if you don't want us to—but do be a sport and let us go with a boatman."

"Try Binns," put in the Funny Man. "He's the man I use. First-class fellow in a whirlpool. Always rows the boat the other way round in a pool so that you can keep quite still and watch it sucking things down. Binns for Brains, I say."

Nobody knew quite how to take this, but Miss Pepper came to the correct conclusion that he was merely being funny. She looked hesitatingly at the beseeching children.

"All right—I'll take you down to the jetty and see you safely into a boat myself with a boatman. In fact, I might even come myself."

"Good," said Roger. "That's settled then. We all go. Barney and Miranda are coming too."

They set off after lunch and met Barney and Miranda. The Funny Man stopped Miss Pepper as they went out.

"Why don't you bring the kids to our show to-night?" he said. "We've got our weekly competition on for children, and one of these might win a prize. Snubby's bright enough anyway! Tell him to bring his banjo and zither. He'll bring the house down with them!"

He walked on. Miss Pepper was surprised. "But you haven't *got* a banjo or a zither, have you, Snubby?" she asked. "What does he mean?"

"Oh, he's just being an ass," said Snubby. "Do let's go to-night, though, Miss Pepper. I'd like to go and see the conjurer anyway."

"And he *does* want to hear Iris Nightingale sing to him," put in Roger, and fled away at top speed as Snubby turned on him.

Miss Pepper found a boatman at the jetty who looked sensible, and strong enough to deal with whirlpools if necessary. She asked him if he could take them.

"Oh, yes, Mam, that's right I can," he said cheerily. "And don't you be afraid of being sucked under, Mam—I can always pull you out again. I got a fine boathook, see?"

This didn't sound too good, but Miss Pepper felt that she couldn't possibly draw back now. So in they all got. Barney and Miranda had joined them by this time, so there was a real boatload.

"Do you mind the dog and the monkey?" said Miss Pepper.

"Not a bit. Only wish I'd brought my parrot. Be a bit of company for her, like," said the boatman with a huge guffaw of laughter. "Here you, lad—take an oar, will you?"

Barney rowed as well as the boatman. They shot out over the little bay and veered to the left.

"The whirlpool is round behind that clump of high rocks there," said the boatman at last. "We go between two sets of dark, high rocks, and then the way opens out—and there we are, on the whirlpool, if so be as I don't stop rowing!"

Loony was a bit of a nuisance. He kept racing from one end of the boat to the other, looking forward at the bows, and backward at the stern. Miranda sat on Barney's shoulder, enjoying the rhythmic to and fro movement as he rowed.

They rounded the clump of high rocks. As they came round them the children saw that there was a narrow, very crooked channel winding between them, down the very middle. It was as if the rocks had been cleft in half, letting the sea run right in.

The high rocks cut off the rays of the sun now and again, as the boat made its way carefully through the

C

winding channel. After a little while the children heard a noise—a boiling, rushing, hissing noise that sounded excited and angry.

"Rubadub Whirlpool," said the boatman. "We goes careful here!"

And carefully they went, feeling a sudden pull on the boat as if the distant pool was putting out suckers to drag them to it!

They rounded a bend slowly—and the boatman slewed the boat quickly round to a ledge where a post stood. In a trice he had thrown a rope over it. The boat was held fast.

The whirlpool was not far from them. The channel had suddenly widened right out into a big rounded pool. It seemed alive and angry. It boiled and bubbled and threw up spray, it swelled up, and then, with a horrible sucking sound, it drained down low. Then up it boiled and bubbled again.

"That's one of the finest whirlpools I ever did see," said the boatman. "And I've seen a-many in my time. Anyone want to get out and walk along the ledge to see the pool properly? I'll show you the rock that gives the name of Rubadub—it's like a scrubbing board."

They all got out eagerly, even Miss Pepper, who was really fascinated by the restless, tortured waters of the strange whirlpool. They climbed up on to the ledge where the mooring-post was, and followed the boatman along another ledge that ran at the side of the high, enclosing rocks.

This ledge led them to a small platform of rock immediately over the pool. From there they had a truly wonderful sight of the boiling, sucking waters. The boatman took a piece of wood up and threw it down into the pool. The waters swelled up, bubbling, and then were sucked under again. When they swelled once more, the piece of wood was nowhere to be seen.

"Sucked down," explained the boatman. "It'll never be seen again. You be careful you don't slip any of you!"

Miss Pepper began to wish they were safely back in the boat, but the old man hadn't finished with them yet.

"Now you watch," he said. "Next time the pool swells up and then goes right down again, look across there to the rocky side opposite. You'll see Rubadub Rock."

They watched the waters swell and subside—down,

down, down—exposing the rock on the other side. And sure enough, it was straight and oblong in shape—and ribbed just like a scrubbing board!

"Old Neptune's scrubbing board," said the boatman. "I guess he used to send the mermaids here to scrub out his best clothes—rubadub-dub!"

"They'd be sucked down!" said Diana with a shudder.

"Oh, they'd like that. That'd be a game to them," said the boatman, enjoying himself. "Do you know what folks say, Missy? They say that in the time of the smugglers and the wreckers, this was a mighty fine place to throw your enemies!"

"Don't!" said Diana. "I shall dream about it to-night! Is there anything else to see?"

"Oh yes—the Blow-Hole!" said the boatman. "I'll show you the Blow-Hole. Follow me—I'll show you something mighty queer."

CHAPTER THIRTEEN

THE BLOW-HOLE

HE TOOK them to the back of the little platform, and walked on another ledge alongside the high rocks. He came to some natural steps in the rocks and climbed up them to the very top of the outcrop of rocks.

It was windy up there. The breeze whipped Diana's hair across her face, and made Miss Pepper clutch at her scarf.

From this rocky height they could see over the Submarine Bay. "You know what goes on there, I don't doubt," said the boatman. "Secret Submarine work. No one's allowed there, not even us fishermen, though as a boy I knew every corner."

A stone enclosure guarded the whole of the bay. No ships could get in or out without the secret openings being unlocked. Men kept guard in little stone shelters along the top. There was a flash from one of them.

"See that?" said the boatman. "That's one of the guards turning his glasses on us. But he knows we can't get farther than this. If you go over the top of these rocks, any nearer the boy, you'll be blown up. They're mined."

This all seems extremely dangerous," said Miss Pepper.

"Bless you, Mam, you couldn't get near the mined bit!" said the boatman reassuringly. "There's hundreds of yards of barbed wire."

"What about the blow-hole?" asked Roger.

"Ah yes. Now—you look over there, see?" said the boatman, and he pointed towards the land, out of which ran the crop of enormous rocks they were standing on.

Suddenly they saw a great spout of water gushing up with a roar. It fell back immediately.

"What was it?" asked Diana, startled.

"I told you. A blow-hole," said the boatman. "Haven't you ever seen one before? There's a-plenty round our coasts, some big, some little. There's a long passage through the rocks from the whirlpool to the blow-hole— and when it's high tide—as it is now—the whirlpool waters get sucked down, and some of them are forced by the tide and the suction through the passage and out of the blow-hole. Watch—there'll be another spout in a minute."

There was. Snubby felt very thrilled. "Why is it only at high tide it comes?" he said. "Why doesn't it come always? Gosh—there goes another! It's like a whale spouting!"

"At low tide the level of the water sinks below the passage," said the boatman. "So no water gets along it. But when high tide swells up the waters again— whoooooosh—they force themselves through the tunnel and out of the blow-hole!"

"Where's the entrance to the passage?" asked Roger. "I suppose it's not visible at high tide?"

"No. Not at all," said the boatman. "But I can show you just about where it is. There's a queer old tale about it."

"What?" asked Snubby at once. He never could resist queer old tales.

"Well, it's said that some smugglers once wanted to get rid of one of their enemies so that his body would never be found again," said the boatman. "And they carried him here at dead of night. They threw him into the whirlpool and fled away, back into the bay over there, where the submarines are now."

He paused, and Snubby urged him on. "Go on—what else?"

"Well, the fellow they threw in was a strong man, a giant of a chap. He wasn't going to be sucked down without a struggle. So, before the waters could suck him right down, he flung himself to the edge of the pool and got a grip on a rocky ledge. But he couldn't haul himself up."

"Did he escape all right?" asked Diana. "Do say he did!"

"The tide went down, and the fellow had to change his grip to lower and lower ledges," said the boatman solemnly. "He couldn't seem to drag himself out, you see. The tide went down and down, and the waters of the whirlpool sank lower and lower. And then the man found himself standing on a ledge at the entrance to what looked like a dark little tunnel in the rocks. I guess it must have been moonlit that night!"

"It was the entrance of the passage that goes to the blow-hole!" said Roger.

"You're right. It was. And up that passage crawled the man right till he came to the blow-hole itself! He scrambled out, made his way back to land—and my word, didn't his enemies stare when they saw him walking down the street. They ran for their lives!"

"I bet they did," said Snubby, enjoying the tale. "Serve them right, the beasts. I hope they all got caught."

"I never heard tell," said the boatman. "There she blows!"

And once again they turned to see the blow-hole send out its sudden high gush of water. "That'll die gradually down as the tide falls," said the boatman. "Well, now, we'll go back. I'm not allowed to take you any farther, and even if I wanted to, there's too many mines about for my liking!"

They watched the blow-hole blow once more and then went back to where they had left the boat. The whirlpool was still performing its endless rhythm, and was boiling away merrily, making a strange, gurgling, groaning, rushing sound.

"Definitely glumpish," said Snubby. "Look at Loony—he's as quiet as a mouse. He's scared, aren't you, Loony-dog?"

Certainly Loony wasn't at all drawn to the whirlpool. He strained away from it as far as ever he could, held tightly on the lead by Snubby.

Miranda was curled up inside Barney's shirt, fast asleep. She didn't even wake when they reached the boat.

"You didn't show us where the entrance hole was," Snubby reminded the boatman.

"No. Nor I didn't," said the man. "Well, while I untie the boat you slip along and look down into the pool. When the water gets sucked down, watch out for a rock with a great knob-like piece on it. The entrance is below that."

Snubby and Roger and Barney went to look. They spotted the knobby rock at once, but could not see any sign of the entrance, of course, because the tide was still very high.

"A jolly interesting afternoon," said Roger. "Kind of trip I like. Something to write about when my form-master gives us his usual essay at beginning of term—'Describe an interesting day in your summer holiday.' I can let myself go about this. I'll put in the tale about the Fellow Who Came Back too. Horrible business it must have been, crawling through that tunnel in the dark—never knowing when the tide might turn and send a long arm of water after you."

"All this has made me hungry," said Snubby. "Anyone got any chocolate?"

Nobody had, so Snubby had to endure his hunger till they reached land. Miss Pepper paid the boatman and they went to have tea at a tea-shop Snubby had spotted that morning.

"It said 'Lobster Teas,'" he explained. "It's just about what I feel like. Why don't we ever have lobster teas at home?"

"Simply because it's easy to catch lobsters by the sea and it isn't inland, idiot," said Roger. "And let me warn you that if you eat more than one lobster you'll probably dream you're being sucked down in that whirlpool to-night."

"It'll be worth it," said Snubby, and was most bitterly disappointed when Miss Pepper refused to let him have more than half a lobster. Miranda liked lobster too. She daintily ate the little bits that Barney held out to her!

They all went for a good walk after tea. They examined

70

the programme for that night's pierrot show as they passed the pier.

"Looks jolly good," said Snubby. "'Fred the Funny Man Keeps You Laughing. Matthew Marvel Mystifies you with Magic. Iris Nightingale sings like her name. Judy Jordan and John Jordan in their Wonderful Dancing Act. Bertram Deep the Baritone, and other talented Players. Philip Drew at the Piano. GREAT WEEKLY CHILDREN'S COMPETITION TO-NIGHT. LET US RECOGNISE YOUR TALENTED CHILDREN EARLY. Two prizes of five shillings.'"

The others read the notice with Snubby. It certainly sounded a good show. They all felt just in the mood for it.

"Super!" said Snubby, rubbing his hands together. "I could do with five shillings. Can't think where my pocket money disappears to."

"Well, I could tell you," began Roger, but Snubby didn't want to hear. "Barney," he said, "if you went on the platform with Miranda, you'd bring the house down."

"I'll be at work, you know that," said Barney.

"Yes, I know. Well, I suppose I'll have to uphold the honour of the family," said Snubby, and began to pretend to play his "banjo" again, making a horrible metallic, buzzing noise between his teeth. "Zizz-ziz-ziz-ziz-ZIZZ, zizz-ziz-ziz-ziz-ZIZZ!"

"*Not* here, please, Snubby," said Miss Pepper. "Is that how you intend to uphold the honour of the family? I shan't know where to look if *you* go up to perform!"

"I prefer your zither," said Diana.

"Or what about my mouth organ?" said Snubby, and pretended to take a mouth organ from his pocket. He wiped it and put it to his mouth. Terrific noise ensued, extremely like a mouth organ. Anyone would really have thought that Snubby was playing one!

"That's *enough*, Snubby," said Miss Pepper, as a little crowd of interested children gathered.

"You know—I could really make a jolly good living at this kind of thing, if I stood at a good corner," said Snubby. "I could put a hat down. I bet it would soon be full of pennies!"

"You're too full of yourself!" said Diana. "Come on—chase Loony and forget all the marvellous things you think you can do—but can't!"

CHAPTER FOURTEEN

AT THE PIERROT SHOW

"I say!" said Snubby, at dinner-time that night, calling across to Iris Nightingale, "I say—we're coming to your show to-night. We'll clap like anything."

"Good," said Iris, smiling at him. She really was very pretty. "We'll put on our very best show for you."

"And be careful to wash your neck, young man, in case I find more potatoes growing there," said Mr. Marvel.

Snubby scowled as everyone laughed. He determined not to give the conjurer one single clap that evening. Mean fellow—talking about unwashed necks in public!

"I'm coming, too, to-night," put in Miss Twitt. "It's the children's competition, isn't it? I do so love seeing the little dears march up on the platform to give their funny little recitations and songs. The pets!"

Snubby's heart sank. He didn't at all like the idea of having Miss Twitt watch his performance. She would be so silly about it afterwards, he was sure.

Miss Twitt turned towards his table and spoke to Miss Pepper with her usual beaming smile. "And are any of your dear children going to perform?" she gushed. "The little girl, now—I'm *sure* she can dance beautifully."

If there was one thing Diana hated it was being called "a little girl." She glanced despairingly at Miss Pepper.

"Do you mean Diana?" said Miss Pepper. "I wonder why you call her a *little* girl, Miss Twitt? She is almost as tall as you are, and very grown-up indeed!"

Diana could have hugged Miss Pepper! She looked at her gratefully. Why didn't all grown-ups know that boys and girls hated to be referred to as "little"?

"Why don't *you* go up and sing on the platform, Miss Twitt?" asked Snubby innocently. "I'm sure you could twitter like a blackbird."

The Funny Man gave a guffaw and turned it into a coughing fit. Miss Pepper looked fiercely at Snubby, but Miss Twitt actually took it as a compliment.

"Well, I *did* sing beautifully as a child," she said coyly. "Fancy you guessing that! He's quite a cute little boy, isn't he?" she said, turning to Miss Pepper.

"You'll have to take Iris's place when she has a night off," said the Funny Man. "You would give everyone a surprise."

"Oh dear no, I couldn't sing like dear Iris," said Miss Twitt, fluttering nervously. "Ah, here comes the pudding —pineapple and ice-cream—how very nice!"

Miss Twitt was usually only silent when she was attacking her food, and the same thing applied to Snubby. Miss Pepper heaved a sigh of relief when she saw the young waiter put a really enormous helping of pineapple and ice-cream in front of Snubby. How did Snubby always get such big helpings? Miss Pepper supposed that, as usual, he made himself well known to the staff, and as so often happened, made himself a firm favourite.

The show began at eight. The Conjurer, the Funny Man, and Iris had coffee quickly and then went to get ready.

"We'll have our coffee in the lounge together, shall we?" said Miss Twitt to Miss Pepper. But Miss Pepper had had quite enough of Miss Twitt.

"I'm not having coffee to-night, thank you," she said. "I'll go and sit outside in the evening sun with the children."

She found them wanting to start off for the show at once. "We do want good seats," said Snubby. "I can't see how a conjurer does his tricks unless I'm right at the front. Miss Pepper, let's go now. Have we got any chocolates to eat?"

"No, we haven't," said Miss Pepper. "There's no need to suck sweets or chocolates at the show—especially after such a good meal."

"Oh well, never mind. I think I've got a piece of chewing-gum," said Snubby, searching his pockets.

"Then please give it to me," said Miss Pepper. "If there's one thing I hate more than another it's to see people's mouths moving up and down, chewing gum— looking exactly like a lot of cows chewing the cud!"

"Gosh! Now I know why cows do that," said Snubby. "It's just as good as chewing-gum to them. I never thought cows could be so sensible. Anyway, Miss Pepper, you don't look at me while I'm chewing."

73

"Shut up, Snubby," said Roger. "You go on and on and on like a babbling brook. Let somebody else get a word in. And keep an eye on Loony. He's disappeared into the inn. He'll be bringing out something he shouldn't, I bet!"

Loony appeared, eagerly wagging his stump of a tail. He was dragging a small mat. He laid it down at Snubby's feet.

"Look at that!" said Snubby in disgust. "He's started his idiotic tricks all over again. Take it back, crazy dog!"

Loony tore off, but without the mat. "Now he's gone to get another!" said Diana. "Miss Pepper, can't we start now?"

"Yes," said Miss Pepper, getting up from the seat. "We'll leave Snubby to cope with the mats."

Snubby snatched up the mat and tore indoors. He collided with the Professor and Miss Twitt inside the hall.

"Oh—sorry," said Snubby. "Frightfully sorry. I didn't see you. Are you going to the show? See you there, then!"

"What that boy wants is a good caning," said the Professor, annoyed. "Always rushing about at top speed, shouting at the top of his voice—no manners at all!"

"Ah, yes—but children *will* be children," said Miss Twitt. "Dear little things. I do so love them, don't you?"

"No, I don't," said the Professor. "I should like to drown them all."

And having made this remark loudly and with much feeling, he said no more, but walked slowly off with Miss Twitt, who jingled and jangled as she went, and left behind her a very strong scent of Sweet Pea perfume.

Snubby soon caught up the others, with Loony tearing at his heels, his ears flapping wildly. He slowed down, panting. They came to the pier turnstiles and paid to go in. Then they made their way to the concert room, which was about half-way down the pier. There was a very good platform, and, in the open air, rows and rows of seats. The roof had been drawn back as it was so warm. In wet or cold weather it could be drawn right across, so that the concert room became an enclosed hall.

"This is fine," said Roger. "Are we going in the very front seats?"

They were all taken, however, so the children had to be content with middle seats in the second row. They sat down expectantly. Miss Pepper bought two programmes between the four of them. They studied them in silence.

Professor James and Miss Twitt joined the audience, but they sat half-way down the hall, as by that time all the front seats were taken. Evidently the Rubadub Rollicks were popular! Miss Twitt waved her programme to the children, and they waved back politely.

At exactly eight o'clock there was the sound of merry music from a piano on the curtained stage. Then the curtains swung back with a flourish, to reveal the twelve Rollicks on the stage, all looking very gay and bright, except for the conjurer, who looked his usual gloomy self. He did, however, manage a smile as they all rose to their feet for the opening song.

The pianist was excellent, a bright young fellow who immediately singled out Snubby, and gave him a broad wink which made Snubby feel very proud.

The programme followed a very usual course—songs, dancing, patter, a little sketch or two, much silly talk from the Funny Man, and, of course, the conjuring.

Iris proved to have a very sweet voice. Snubby clapped her so hard that his hands felt quite sore. He went on clapping long after everyone else had stopped. Roger poked him hard with his elbow.

"Shut up! Everyone's looking at you!"

"Encore!" shouted Snubby, undeterred. "Encore!" He was delighted when, at a word from the Funny Man, Iris got up to sing again. She gave him an amused smile.

The ordinary dancing was quite good, and the tap-dancing excellent. Snubby began to strum on his imaginary banjo when Judy Jordan began a tricky little tap dance with clicking toes and heels. Miss Pepper stopped him at once, hearing the familiar "Zizz-ziz-ziz" beginning.

But the best part of the whole show was the conjurer. He was quite brilliant. He didn't smile once as he went through his ritual, dressed for the act as an old-time Enchanter, with pointed hat and flowing cloak. He made Diana shudder, as with gloomy face and deep, gloomy voice he performed his act.

"He's really excellent," Miss Pepper whispered to Diana. "Absolutely in character with his magic! You could imagine him conjuring up genies and spirits and hob-nobbing with witches and goblins. He's really weird!"

The audience watched him in silence. He did unusual tricks. He picked most extraordinary things out of the air—a rose-spray—a pack of loose cards—quite a large book—a bonnet, which he presented to Iris with a deep bow!

He took his wand and announced that he was about to conjure up fire. He muttered a string of queer words that sent shivers down Snubby's spine—and then, hey presto! flames sprang up above his head, burning brilliantly. He really did the most extraordinary things!

"And now," he said, putting down his wand, "now I propose to show you my wonderful mind-reading act. Magic, my friends, pure magic!"

CHAPTER FIFTEEN

MR. MARVEL—AND SNUBBY

"You watch this," whispered somebody in the seats behind the three children. "It's marvellous!"

Iris stepped forward and bowed. Apparently she was to be Mr. Marvel's assistant. "Blindfold me," commanded the conjurer. Iris took a very large black scarf and blindfolded Mr. Marvel well and truly. Even Snubby was absolutely sure that nobody could see a thing under that scarf. It made the conjurer look very sinister indeed!

The mind-reading act followed the usual ritual. Iris collected articles from the audience, walking down the rows of chairs, smiling, putting her fingers to her lips.

"Mustn't give anything away!" she whispered. "No hints, nothing that might help Mr. Marvel. This is a true and honest test of his powers!"

She went back to the stage. Mr. Marvel, still blindfolded, was twisted round by Iris so that he stood with his back to the audience. She stepped to the front and held out a little gold brooch, given to her by a young girl.

"What do I hold in my hand, Mr. Marvel?" she cried. "Tell me! Let your mind read what I hold!"

Mr. Marvel began to swing his great cloak so that it flowed round him like black waves. He began to mutter in a deep, growly voice that made Loony, who was fast asleep under Snubby's chair, wake up at once.

"I see—what do I see—mirrity-marrity-mingle-o—I see, ah yes, I see—something small—something round—something that shines like gold—abblety-gabblety-mingle-o—it IS gold!"

"Ah, but what is it?" cried Iris, still holding up the little brooch. There wasn't a sound in the concert hall, as Mr. Marvel began to mutter again. He suddenly swung right round, his cloak flying out round him.

"A brooch. A little brooch!"

There was a loud storm of clapping. Snubby forgot that he didn't mean to clap, and clapped hard; Roger and Diana clapped even harder than Snubby. Then Iris swung Mr. Marvel round with his back to the audience again, and this time she held up two things for them to see. One was a silver ring with a yellow stone in it and one was a watch.

"What do I hold now, Mr. Marvel?" cried Iris. "Two things I hold for your mind to read. Tell me what they are!"

There was muttering and mumbling again, and the cloak swung this way and that. To the three children it all seemed very weird and magical indeed. Mr. Marvel brought the house down by guessing both articles quite correctly. He waited till the applause had died down and then said:

"Wait—I see something else. The watch, I see the watch —on the back it has the letters A.G.S. Yes, I see A.G.S."

"You're quite right," said Iris in an astonished voice, looking at the back of the watch. Every one clapped again. A few more articles were held up and correctly described, and then came the last part of the magician's act.

"And now," said Mr. Marvel solemnly, his long thin face looking even longer beneath his pointed hat, "now we come to Numerology. My excellent assistant, Miss Iris, has a pack of cards with her. Each card bears a high number. She will shuffle the cards and pick one at random, showing it to you in silence. I will see it in my mind's eye within thirty seconds or less, and tell you the number she holds in her hand."

Iris took up a pack of cards. They all had plain-coloured backs of yellow. Snubby sat up suddenly. Why, these were the cards that he had seen in the conjurer's room when he had taken back his hair-brush. He must have been studying them then. But what good would any study do if he didn't know which one Iris was going to pick out?

Iris picked out a card and held it up silently. The number on it was printed in black ink, in large figures across the card. Everyone could see perfectly. The number was 673589255.

The usual muttering noise came from Mr. Marvel. Then he groaned. "It is difficult. Where's my wand?"

Iris gave it to him. He made various passes with it in the air. "Come, genie of the numbers, come to my aid!" he cried, in such an anguished voice that the audience felt scared.

"Ah! AH! Now I see the number! Wait, wait—it comes! The number is 673589255!"

Iris was still holding up the number. Mr. Marvel had guessed it correctly. There was a shout of applause, and clapping and stamping of feet. Wonderful!

"Let's have another number!" shouted a voice.

"Only one more," said Iris. "This is a great strain on Mr. Marvel."

It certainly seemed to be by his writhings and mutterings and passes in the air with his wand. But he at last guessed the number correctly again.

"It is—it is—864592643!"

"Gosh—he scares me," said Snubby to Miss Pepper. "I'm going to be jolly polite to him in future. He's a wonder."

There was a merry song and dance next, to remove the tense atmosphere that Mr. Marvel had so cleverly created. Then Iris stepped forward again.

"Now comes the end of our programme and perhaps the best part," she said with her engaging smile. "The Children's Competition. As usual we have two prizes of five shillings, one for the cleverest boy, and one for the cleverest girl."

A jingling noise from the Funny Man proclaimed that the money was ready and waiting. "Can I go in for it, please, Miss?" said the Funny Man pathetically. "I can sing 'Three Blind Mice' well, I can, really."

Iris went on with her little speech. "We don't mind what you do—sing, dance, recite, play our piano, tell us a funny story—or even do a bit of conjuring that will put Mr.

Marvel into the shade. Now come along—who will be first?"

Two small girls and a boy pushed their way eagerly to the stage. Another girl followed, and two more boys. Roger gave Snubby a nudge. "Go on! Do your stuff too, Snubby."

But Snubby was unaccountably overcome with nerves, and he glowered at Roger. "I'm not going to make a fool of myself, so shut up."

The children proved very ordinary indeed. Two of the girls played the piano, thumping hard and strong. One boy sang a comic song, of which nobody could hear a single word.

Another small girl did a competent little step dance, but was obviously so conceited that nobody clapped very much except her fond and admiring Mamma.

Then a boy about Snubby's age gave a recitation at top speed so that nobody could follow it at all. He then retired from the platform, also at top speed quite overcome by his effort.

The third boy refused to perform after all. He stood up on the platform the picture of misery.

"I've forgot me words," he kept saying. "I've forgot me words. Mum, what's me words?"

Mum had apparently forgotten them, too, so the small boy left the platform in tears.

"Now now, children!" said Iris reprovingly. "I'm *sure* there's somebody else who can try for the five shillings. We do badly want another boy."

"Let *me* try, Miss, do let *me* try," urged the Funny Man, putting on a little-boy voice. "I'm top of my form, I am, for singing and whistling." He pursed up his mouth to whistle, but hard as he blew, no sound came. So he produced a big whistle from his pocket and blew, making Iris jump violently. Everyone laughed, he was so idiotic.

"One more boy!" urged Iris. "Just one. Then we shall have had three girls performing and three boys."

The Funny Man came to stand beside Iris. He looked straight at Snubby. Then he pointed at him. "Look, Iris," he said, "there's the World's Wonder down there. See him? Chap with red hair, turned-up nose and freckles! Finest banjo player the world has even seen. Pays a hundred pounds for each of his banjos. Whew!"

Every one craned their necks to look at Snubby. He went scarlet to the roots of his red hair. "Come on, son!" cried the Funny Man. "Come on up and play your banjo. Tell us your tune and the pianist will accompany you."

"Go on, Snubby," said Roger. "You've got to, now. Those other boys were frightful."

Snubby went up to the platform, half annoyed, half pleased at the Funny Man's patter. He stood facing the audience. The Funny Man solemnly placed a chair beside him. "To put your leg up on," he informed him. "That's a heavy banjo you have there. Rest it on your leg, mate. Now—what's your tune?"

Snubby suddenly entered into the fun of it. He laughed. "I'll play you 'What's the time when it's twelve o'clock,'" he announced, and put his leg on the chair. The song was very popular just then, a silly jigging tune, admirable for the banjo. The pianist nodded. He knew the tune well.

"I must just tune up," said Snubby, and he solemnly tuned up the strings of his imaginary banjo, making twanging noises as if he really were screwing the wires to their correct pitch. People began to laugh.

"Right. Ready?" said Snubby to the pianist. "Not too loud, please. Tune all through, the chorus twice."

He brought his hand down on imaginary strings and made a startling twanging noise. Then off he went, twanging away with his right hand, and with his mouth making a most remarkable banjo-like noise he followed the tune absolutely correctly. Snubby could make his noises very loudly, and the pianist did not drown him at all, but followed him perfectly. They made an excellent pair.

"Twang-a-twang-twang-twang, twang-a-twang-twang," went Snubby, and ended off with what sounded like a marvellous chord. He put down his leg and bowed solemnly.

He got more applause than any other member of the show had been given, even more than Mr. Marvel! Every-one yelled for more.

"One more—can you manage it?" asked the Funny Man, delighted. "Any other instrument?"

"I've happened to bring my zither," said Snubby solemnly, and put down his imaginary banjo and took up his imaginary zither. "I'll have to sit down for this, please."

He sat down, and once more he and the pianist gave an extraordinary performance together. Snubby reproduced the harp-like sounds of a zither perfectly, and instead of a jiggy song, he chose a romantic tune, "If I could only give you the moon." He didn't sing it, of course, but made the sound of a zither playing the tune. It was most remarkable. Everyone listened intently.

Fancy *Snubby*, the crazy idiotic *Snubby* holding a big audience like this with just a little make-believe! Roger and Diana felt swollen up with pride in their cousin!

The tune ended. The Funny Man bowed to Snubby. "Quite a maestro!" he said, and Snubby wondered whether he was being rude or complimentary. He had never heard the word before. But the Funny Man was delighted with him. He turned to the audience. "And now to give out the prizes," he said. "We award the girl's prize to little Lorna Jones for her step dancing."

There was very slight applause. Certainly Lorna had been good, but nobody had liked the little show-off.

"The boy's prize goes—of course—to our young friend here, for . . ."

But the rest of his words were drowned in claps and stamps and cheers. Snubby, redder than ever, bowed, and took the five shillings. What an evening! Whoever would have thought that his crazy habit of strumming imaginary musical instruments would have brought Snubby such applause?

CHAPTER SIXTEEN

WHAT HAPPENED IN THE NIGHT

SNUBBY walked home in a whirl of excitement. "Now don't let all this go to your head," said Roger, afraid that Snubby might become quite unbearable. "After all, you can't *really* play the banjo or the zither—and you can only pick out 'chop-sticks' on the piano. You're no musician, really."

"And for goodness' sake don't play banjos and things all over the hotel," begged Diana. "They won't like it a bit if you do."

Snubby took not the slightest notice. "I've been wondering if I could do an organ," he said. "Or a drum."

"*No*, Snubby," said Miss Pepper firmly. "Oh dear, here comes Miss Twitt. Hurry!"

But Miss Twitt was determined to pile praises on Snubby. "The little wonder!" she said, as she hurried up to them. "What a little marvel! The clever little boy. He's a born player, isn't he, Miss Pepper?"

"Well—I wouldn't say *that*," said Miss Pepper. "He can't play a note, actually."

"Fancy that! It just shows how wonderful he is to make people think he *can* play!" prattled Miss Twitt. "I *quite* thought it was a real banjo, you know. He really *ought* to join the pierrots, oughtn't he? Everyone would come to hear him!"

Miss Pepper glanced at Snubby and was horrified to see a pleased and fatuous smile on his face. He was drinking it all in!

"Snubby's little tricks are quite all right to amuse his friends at school," she said firmly. "But that's really all they are. It's silly to think them anything else, Miss Twitt."

Fortunately they had now reached the inn. "I want a drink," announced Snubby. "All that twang-a-twang has made me thirsty. Can I have a lemonade, Miss Pepper—two if you like. Oh, I say—wait a bit, though—I'd forgotten my five shillings. Drinks all round, please. What'll you have, Miss Pepper? Miss Twitt? Orangeade? Lemonade? Or go a splash and have a ginger beer?"

Diana began to giggle. Snubby really could be very funny. Miss Pepper ordered the drinks and then sent all three children, and a very sleepy Loony, up to bed.

"It's late," she said. "Very late. Take your orangeade with you. No, Snubby, I don't care if you have five shillings or ten shillings, you can't have more than one orangeade. No, Loony can't have one either. Water is good enough for him."

Snubby went off sorrowfully. He had hoped to stay downstairs until Iris, Mr. Marvel and the Funny Man came back, and also Professor James who had still not returned. Praise from them would be worth a hundred times more than fulsome words from Miss Twitt.

Snubby was too excited to go to sleep that night. Roger snored gently and peacefully while Snubby tossed and turned, his mind full of wonderful plans. He would practise more and more imaginary instruments to play. He would broadcast—perhaps he wouldn't though, because people might think he was *really* playing a banjo or zither or guitar—they wouldn't be able to *see* that he hadn't really got one.

Well, what about television, then? That would be the thing. And what about a drum? He was sure he could make that big BOOM-BOOM noise. He began to practise it very softly. Then he couldn't resist doing a very loud BOOM!

And then a most frightening thing happened. As soon as Snubby had delivered his BOOM, another BOOM came—a terrific one, muffled and very frightening. The inn shook. Snubby sat up in bed, scared.

"Bombs!" he thought. "No—can't be. Of course—it's an explosion in the Submarine Bay. Some experiment like the one we heard the other day."

He thought for a moment. "But wait a minute—this is the middle of the night—about half-past two, I should think. They wouldn't experiment then, and wake everyone up."

The noise hadn't however, awakened Roger, who was in his deepest sleep. It hadn't awakened Diana either. Miss

Pepper had heard it, and had sat up, listening. But as there was no more sound she had lain down again.

Snubby felt restless. He couldn't possibly lie down and go to sleep to-night. A thought flashed into his head. He would go up that little stairway that led to the skylight, open it, and peer our. He *might* be able to see something through that cleft in the cliff—something down in the Submarine Bay!

He slipped out of bed and went to the door. He opened it and went out on to the dark landing. Nobody seemed to be stirring. Perhaps they hadn't heard the noise then.

Snubby stole to the little door that shut off the steep staircase. He opened it quietly. "Yes—there was the staircase—he could feel it with his foot though he couldn't see it. He went up cautiously. It was a clear night and Snubby could see stars shining through the little square of glass set in the middle of the trap-door that opened on to the roof.

He opened it, pushing it back carefully, so as not to make a sound. He looked out.

Gosh! Something *had* happened down in the Submarine Bay. Snubby could see quite clearly through the cleft in the cliff. Far away, on the other side of it, was the bay, and something was burning there, on the water. Searchlights were playing here and there. Snubby held his breath. Something had happened. Some awful accident, perhaps. He wished he could see more.

"Perhaps if I climb right out of the trap-door I can find a higher place to see from," he thought. "It would be easy."

He climbed to the topmost stair and found it simple to get out on the roof, which, just there, was flat. Snubby looked round. There was a rise in the roof just to the right of him, where a set of chimneys rose up together. He could sit on the little rise, beside a chimney.

He made his way cautiously across the rise in the roof, and crawled up it on hands and knees. Now he was by a chimney. But the wind swept him that side, so he crawled round in between two chimneys where he was well protected. One chimney was warm—good!

But to his disappointment he couldn't see much more of the bay than he had seen before, although he was now a little higher. Searchlights were still criss-crossing, and the flames of whatever was burning were still as high. Perhaps a submarine had exploded and was on fire.

Snubby cuddled up to the warm chimney, feeling daring to be out on the roof in the middle of the night. He suddenly sniffed the air.

He could smell something. What was it? Cigarette smoke! Couldn't be! No one else was up on the roof in the middle of the night—smoking a cigarette too!

He craned his neck round the chimney, and saw, in the distance, a tiny glow, the red, burning end of somebody's cigarette. Somebody else had heard the explosion then and had come to see what could be seen.

He soon saw that the glowing end was just where the trap-door opened on to the roof. Somebody must be standing on the stairs there, looking out and smoking. Snubby was just about to give a low call to tell them that he, too, was there, and had heard everything, when he stopped himself.

No. He'd get into a frightful row for being out on the roof at night. If Miss Pepper heard of it she would be furious. There wouldn't be any second helpings for the rest of the holidays! Silence was best. But *who* was it there? Snubby screwed up his eyes, but he could only make out a blob of a head with the glowing end of the cigarette in front.

After a while the smoker finished his cigarette and threw it down the roof. Snubby heard the soft creak of the stairs. Somebody was going down them—but that somebody had shut down the trap-door first! Snubby's heart missed a beat or two. He could imagine himself sitting out on the roof all night—falling asleep—rolling down the roof—oh, how simply horrible!

He crept across to the trap-door. As he got there, a light sprang in the window of a room some distance away. Snubby stopped. Who was in there? Probably, whoever it was, was the smoker of a few minutes before—he must have returned to his room and switched on his light. Snubby decided to see who it was.

He crawled to another position, and found that he could look right across the roof into the lighted room. The curtains were drawn across, but there was a space about a foot left in the middle.

"Gosh! It's old Professor James!" said Snubby. "What

a good thing I didn't let him know I was up here. He'd have told Mrs. Glump and Miss Pepper and got me into an awful row!"

He tried the trap-door with a trembling hand. Had the Professor slipped the catch into place, so that it could not be opened?

With an enormous sigh of relief Snubby found that he *could* open it. Thank goodness! He swung it back, and then clambered on to the narrow wooden stairway. He closed the trap-door quietly and then climbed down the stairs. He opened the door at the bottom, went on to the landing and back to his room. Roger was still fast asleep.

Just as he was about to shut his door he saw a line of light under a door nearby. It was Mr. Marvel's door. So he had heard the explosion too. Snubby debated whether to go in and have a chat about it—surely Mr. Marvel would welcome him now that he had given such a fine performance in the show!

He decided against it, however. Mr. Marvel wasn't quite the person to enjoy a midnight chat. He might start to do a bit more unpleasant magic on Snubby.

CHAPTER SEVENTEEN

THE NEXT DAY

IN THE morning the whole inn was agog with the news of the explosion in the night. So were the papers.

"GREAT EXPLOSION IN HUSH-HUSH BAY," said the headlines. "WAS IT SABOTAGE? ARE OUR SECRETS SAFE? INHABITANTS OF SURROUNDING TOWNS ALMOST HURLED FROM THEIR BEDS."

"What a lie!" said Snubby. "The bed just shook that's all. And you didn't even wake, Roger. I did."

"Did you?" said Roger. "Was it really a big explosion?"

"Terrific," said Snubby. "Tremendous. Louder than

thunder. I got out of bed and went up that stairway to
look out of the trap-door—and I saw something burning
like anything. And searchlights going like mad over the
bay."

"Sh! Miss Pepper will hear you," said Diana. "She'd be
furious if she thought you went wandering about at night—
especially up to the roof."

"She didn't hear," said Snubby. He glanced round. Old
Professor James was nearby reading a newspaper. He was
deaf so he wouldn't have heard either. Mr. Marvel and
the Funny Man were also near—they would have heard,
but probably they didn't know about the staircase anyway.

"I did something else too," said Snubby, lowering his
voice. "I got out on the roof and sat beside a jolly warm
chimney. Somebody else came up the staircase and looked
out too. The old Professor, I think. Fancy him hearing the
explosion and not you, Roger!"

"I expect the vibration woke him, not the noise," said Diana. "I say—it's pretty serious, isn't it? One of our newest submarines blown up to the surface—and then burnt to nothing! I do wish you'd woken me up, Snubby!"

"You'd have hated seeing it," said Snubby. "Is it sabotage, do you think? I mean—would it be possible for anyone to get into the bay and do a thing like that to damage us? I should have thought things were much too strict and closely guarded."

"It was probably an accident," said Roger. "You can't have successful experiments without accidents. Look at the things that happen in the lab. at school!"

"Oh well—we *plan* some of those," said Snubby. "A bit of well-planned trickery! All the same—I'd like to know if it *was* an accident. I don't want to think of people somewhere around planning to blow up more submarines—especially while we're staying here."

"Why? Are you afraid of being mixed up in another mystery?" asked Roger with a grin.

"*Afraid!*" said Snubby with scorn. "I *like* mysteries. I dote on them. But this isn't a mystery, it seems to me. I bet it's an accident."

Whether it was or not they didn't learn from any of the papers that morning or evening. The Press seemed to shut down on the incident, which annoyed the children very much.

That afternoon was wet. The rain poured down and the children looked gloomy.

"It's a glumpish afternoon," said Snubby. "What shall we do? Shall I practise my banjo?"

"Not unless you go up on the roof or somewhere far away," said Roger. Snubby had produced his imaginary banjo, zither, guitar and harp at different times that day, and Roger and Diana were getting a little tired of the remarkable twanging, zizzing, buzzing sounds produced by Snubby.

"Let's go up that little stairway and see if the poor old submarine is still burning," said Snubby. "I promise I won't take any musical instruments with me!"

They ran upstairs to their landing and went to the little door that enclosed the staircase. Snubby turned the handle. But the door wouldn't open!

"What's the matter with it? Is it stuck?" he said, and

pulled violently. All that happened was that the handle came completely off in his hand and he sat down heavily on a startled Loony.

"Ass! You *would* do that!" said Roger.

"Things always come off in my hand," complained Snubby. "Now what shall we do?"

"You'll have to go and own up to Mrs. Glump," said Diana. "Go on, Snubby. If you were brave enough to get out and sit on the roof last night, surely you're brave enough to confess to Mrs. Glump."

So Snubby had to go and find Mrs. Glump. She was in a peculiar little den, adding up rows and rows of figures, and didn't look at all pleased to see Snubby. He explained what had happened.

"But why did you pull at the handle so violently?" asked Mrs. Glump, resting her face on her four or five chins, and looking most majestic. Snubby wished he had a few chins he could look majestic with too. He felt very small beside Mrs. Glump, and she made him feel like a naughty little boy.

"Well, I pulled hard because the door stuck," said Snubby. "It's locked, I think."

"Locked! But the key would be in the lock anyway," said Mrs. Glump.

"There wasn't a key. I looked," said Snubby. "I'm sure it's locked, Mrs. Glump. I thought *you* must have locked it. I'm sorry about the handle. I've still got one and six-pence left out of the five shillings I won at the pierrot show yesterday. Would one and six pay for a new handle?"

"I expect so," said Mrs. Glump. "But I'm sure Dummy has an old one he could fix on quickly. Go and ask him. And I hear I must congratulate you on winning the prize yesterday. Let me see—you played the banjo, didn't you?"

"Not a real one. My imaginary one. Paid a hundred pounds for it!" said Snubby with a grin, and immediately began to play a jigging, strident tune, twang-twanging in a most lifelike manner.

Mrs. Glump began to laugh. She had a very curious laugh. It seemed to begin somewhere deep down and then rumbled all the way past her magnificent chins, and came out as a very hearty affair indeed.

Snubby stopped, bowed and grinned. "You're a caution," said Mrs. Glump. "Get on with you! Go and find

Dummy about the handle. And don't shut my door too violently in case the whole door comes off in your hand."

Snubby went out, pleasantly surprised. She wasn't really glumpish at all! He made his way to the kitchen to find Dummy. He was polishing some horse-brasses one by one and making a very good job of them.

"Hallo, Dummy. Can I help you? I collect horse-brasses too," said the cheerful Snubby. "I say, did you hear about me winning the five bob at the show last night?"

Dummy listened and nodded. "You," he said. "You win. Good boy."

"My word, you *are* a chatterbox to-day," said Snubby, rubbing vigorously at a brass.

"What you do?" asked Dummy earnestly.

"This," said Snubby, and played his imaginary banjo again. To his enormous surprise, Dummy also picked up an imaginary banjo and began to twang it, making a most peculiar noise as he did so, almost as good as Snubby's!

"Here—what's all this?" said a voice, and the face of the young waiter poked round the door. "Some band performing here?"

Dummy fled at once, out into the back-yard. He sat down, blinking his eyes, confused. Years and years ago he had had a real banjo and he could play it. But when he had fallen from the rope, during a wire-walking act, he had hurt his head—and after that Dummy was different. Poor Dummy!

He sat till his mind cleared a little. He began to smile. Yes—he remembered his old banjo—and the tunes he played. He twanged imaginary strings again.

Snubby came into the yard to find him. "Oh, there you are, Dummy. I say, I forgot to tell you what I wanted you for. Have you got a spare door-handle? I've somehow pulled off the handle of the door that shuts in that little stairway leading to the roof."

"Roof," said Dummy. He stared at Snubby and then suddenly leaned forward. He whispered loudly in his ear. "Mind bad men up there! Bad men!"

Snubby drew back, startled. Dummy smiled and nodded at him. Then his face grew solemn again. "Bad, bad, bad," he whispered again. "Dummy see. Dummy watch. Dummy follow. Bad!"

Snubby looked at Dummy doubtfully. Poor old fellow—

what peculiar imaginings had he got now? He couldn't imagine Dummy watching people and stalking them! Snubby decided to humour him.

"Snubby see. Snubby watch. Snubby follow," he said, equally solemnly. "Gosh, we sound like Red Indians or something. Dummy, where's an old door-handle? Let's find one and go in. I'm not too keen on sitting out here in the rain—twang-a-twang-twang-twang, zizz-a-zizz-ziz-ziz. Ker-plonk! There—I knew a string would bust if I played out in the rain. See that?"

He held out his imaginary banjo, and Dummy laughed delightedly. It was the first time Snubby had heard him laugh. It was a ripple, just like a very young child's. Snubby patted Dummy on the back.

"That's right. Laugh your troubles away! Have you got a door-handle, for the third time of asking?"

Dummy had. He produced one from a shed and went upstairs. He was clever with his fingers and had soon fixed it on the door. He gave it a pull.

"Locked," said Snubby. "And the key's gone. Who did that? And why? I tell you, Dummy, there were mysterious goings on up here last night!"

"Indeed? And what were they?" said a voice.

Snubby jumped and turned round. Mr. Marvel the conjurer was standing outside his door. Snubby thought furiously. No—he wasn't going to give anything away and get himself into trouble.

"Oh, nothing," he said airily. "I was just putting the wind up old Dummy. I say, sir—that was a wizard act you put on last night. How did you guess those articles—and the initials on the back of the watch? Beats me!"

"That's *my* secret," said Mr. Marvel. "Did you hear the explosion last night?"

"Yes, I jolly well did," said Snubby. "Did you?"

"No, I didn't," said Mr. Marvel, which surprised Snubby very much. Hadn't he seen a line of light under Mr. Marvel's door when he, Snubby, had come down from the roof to go to bed again?

"I saw a light under your door though," blurted out Snubby, and could have kicked himself.

"Indeed? And what were *you* doing out on the landing at that time of night?" said Mr. Marvel at once.

"Just peeped out to see if any one was awake after the

91

explosion," said Snubby. "I say, sir—how *did* you guess those numbers last night?"

But Mr. Marvel was gone. Snubby was left staring at a closing door. He made a face at it. All right—*be* snooty, Mr. Marvel! You *were* awake last night! Snubby shook a furious fist, marched into his own room, and slammed the door!

CHAPTER EIGHTEEN

THE TIME GOES BY

AFTER THE first few days the holidays began to slip away fast, as holidays always do.

A week had gone by before any of the children realised it. It had been a good week—bathing, boating, paddling, walking—messing about with Barney and Miranda. Loony had enjoyed himself too.

He dug violently every morning, covering everyone with sand. He then ran into the sea and got thoroughly wet. Then he came back and shook himself really vigorously, showering everyone with drops of sea water.

He had also developed a new and most irritating habit. Having been smacked hard for attempting to bring brushes, towels and mats on to the beach, he cast about for something that nobody could possibly object to.

He brought along a strange dog each day to play with him. The first time he brought a peculiar-looking mongrel with very short legs and a large head.

"Look at that," said Snubby. "Poor creature. If its legs were much shorter they wouldn't touch the ground!"

"Ha ha—very old joke," said Diana. "All the same, it *is* a peculiar dog."

"It's a bit of a smelly dog," said Roger, as the dog sat down heavily on his legs. "Get off, Smelly! Go away!"

But Smelly had no intention of leaving his good friend Loony. They went crazy together and nearly drove Miss Pepper mad as they tore round and round her deck-chair. They had to put up with Smelly all day, and were amazed to see Loony sharing all his tit-bits with him.

The next day Loony trotted off the beach and returned with a second friend—a bulldog with a face a bit like Mr. Tubby's. He wasn't as bad as Smelly, and he liked to sit as near every one as possible.

"I wish you wouldn't *dribble* all over me," Snubby said to the bulldog. "You want a bib or something. Miss Pepper do bulldogs always dribble or is this one just doing it on purpose?"

"He's dribbled over me too," said Diana. "I remember a teacher at school who had a bulldog and he dribbled as well. Loony, next time you bring a friend, bring one who doesn't smell *or* dribble!"

The bulldog was very sweet-tempered until he took a fancy to a bone that Loony was gnawing. Then he gave out such blood-curdling growls that even Snubby drew back. Miranda was with them at the time and she leapt on the top of Barney's head in fright.

"Go away," said Miss Pepper firmly to bulldog. "That's Loony's bone. Go away!"

The bulldog calmly picked up the bone and waddled off. Snubby gave Loony a poke with his foot.

"Coward dog! Couldn't keep his own bone! Cowardy custard!"

Loony hung his head. He crept off the beach when no one was looking. He returned looking quite a different dog, bright and cheerful, accompanied by three small dogs of the terrier type, all very alert and inquisitive.

"Oh, stop it, Loony! Have you gone potty?" said Snubby, surveying the four dogs in disgust. "What do you want to go and pick up half the town for? Shoo! Scat! Clear off, all of you. No, not you, Loony. You're going to be tied up to Miss Pepper's deck-chair for the rest of the day."

"Oh no, he's not," said Miss Pepper at once. "You did that two days ago and he made my chair collapse. Tie him to your foot!"

Barney was rather quiet after three or four days. He didn't encourage the others to go to the fair. "It's a rough place," he said. "Don't come. I don't like the men who run it either. They're cheats. They're in some racket or other, too, but I don't know what it is."

"Why don't you leave them, Barney?" said Diana

anxiously. "I *knew* you weren't pleased with the job. Don't stay with dishonest men."

"Oh, I'm used to that type," said Barney. "You can't knock about as I do without coming up against them all the time. Anyway—where would I get another job?"

"Don't you remember—the conjurer belonging to the pierrot show said he'd take you as an assistant," said Diana, remembering.

"But he's got Iris," said Snubby. "I don't know why he said he wanted another assistant!"

"No. Perhaps he doesn't," said Diana. "When's your week up, Barney? To-morrow, isn't it?"

"Yes. I get paid then," said Barney. "Two whole pounds! I can buy some new sandshoes and a shirt."

"Well, *do* leave then," said Diana. "I don't like that place either. I'm *sure* you could get a job somewhere else!"

But Barney wouldn't say he would leave. It wouldn't be easy to get another job in Rubadub, and he did so want to be near his friends.

That night Iris didn't go to the show. It was her night off. She sat in the lounge and played cards with the children, looking almost as young as Diana. Snubby sat next to her, wishing he could deal her the best cards in the pack. Loony sat on her feet. He agreed with his master that Iris was a very nice girl indeed.

"What will Mr. Marvel do without you to-night?" asked Diana, watching Roger deal the cards. "Does he do his mind-reading act when you're not there to help?"

"I don't know," said Iris. "I don't care either! Surly fellow. I don't like him."

"Why?" asked Snubby.

But Iris wouldn't tell why. "He used to have a helper," she said. "A youngish fellow. Then he suddenly went, I never knew why, and Mr. Marvel asked me to take over till he got someone else. I said I'd try for two weeks. But I don't like it, and I'm not doing it any more. The two weeks are up now."

Diana now knew why Mr. Marvel had asked Barney to be his helper. He had been afraid that Iris wouldn't go on with him after two weeks.

"Has he got anyone instead of you, do you know?" she asked suddenly.

"Someone came to see him to-day. I expect he was after

94

the job," said Iris. "He'll probably get it, too, because Mr. Marvel must have someone. He can't do that mind-reading act without an assistant."

"Why not?" asked Snubby. "Anyone from the audience could be called up—or one of the other pierrots."

"No. He wants a proper assistant of his own," said Iris. "Look, are we playing a game of cards or is this just a chatter party? I've got such a wonderful hand that I'm longing to play it!"

Diana didn't play very well that night. She was thinking hard. Suppose they went to Mr. Marvel and begged him to take Barney instead of the other applicant? If they could tell Barney they had the job for him, surely he would give notice at the little fair to-morrow, and join the pierrots? He would make a wonderful assistant!

She could hardly wait to tell the others when they went to bed that night. They listened in silence.

"Yes," said Roger. "I think we ought to tell Mr. Marvel that Barney doesn't like his job, and will he take him instead of the other fellow, whoever he is. But *you'd* better ask him, Di. You're better at that kind of thing. You catch him all alone to-morrow morning and put your case!"

So, the next morning, when breakfast was over, Diana went to look for Mr. Marvel. He was sitting in a garden shelter, reading the paper. He looked up as she came shyly in.

"Please can I speak to you, Mr. Marvel?" she said. "It's about that friend of ours, Barney. He doesn't like his job. I'm sure he'd come as your assistant if you still want one. Please have him instead of any one else. He's a very hard worker and very clever. He'd do *anything* you want him to, anything."

Mr. Marvel put down his paper and looked at the earnest Diana. "I'm looking for a *servant*, really," he said. "Someone who will do errands for me, see after my clothes, take messages, as well as help in my act."

"He could do all that," said Diana eagerly. "Do try him, Mr. Marvel."

"What's his full name?" asked the conjurer, taking out a fountain pen and notebook.

"Barnabas Hugo Lorimer," said Diana. "Actually that's his mother's name. He doesn't know his father's."

"How strange," said Mr. Marvel.

Diana plunged into Barney's story, and Mr. Marvel listened with interest. "So you see," finished Diana, "Barney is all alone in the world, he can go where he likes and take what job he likes—but oh, I *do* wish he could find his father!"

"I've no doubt I could do that for him!" said Mr. Marvel, putting away his fountain pen. Diana gasped and stared.

"What do you mean? How could you? How would you set about it? Surely you couldn't, if even Barney doesn't know anything about his father—not even his name!"

"My dear young lady, I have been in the theatrical world for more years than I like to remember," said Mr. Marvel. "I have only to ask a few of my friends if they knew of a Shakespearian actor some fifteen or so years ago, who is probably very like Barney in feature—he has a most remarkable face, that boy. I'm quite certain I shall have news within a very short time!"

"Oh, Mr. Marvel!" cried Diana, her eyes shining. "Oh, it would be wonderful! Will you really do that?"

"If Barney comes to me, does what he is told and proves himself useful and trustworthy, then I shall certainly do my best," said Mr. Marvel. "It rests with the boy himself. I'm not likely to take any trouble though, unless he does well with me."

"Oh, Barney will do well, I know he will!" cried Diana joyfully. "Let me go and fetch him, Mr. Marvel. Then he can give in his notice to-day, and come to you to-morrow. Oh, thank you, thank you."

She flew off, her heart singing. Oh, Barney, Barney, suppose your father is found quite soon! Oh, wonderful Mr. Marvel, kind Mr. Marvel—why had she ever thought she disliked him?

She found Barney down on the beach, waiting for her and the others. She flopped down beside him and told him her news. "Please go to the inn now, this very minute, Barney!" she begged. "He's there, waiting for you. Barney, just suppose he really *can* find your father for you! He seemed quite certain he would!"

"You're a good friend, Diana," said Barney, his eyes shining. "Come on, Miranda—we'll go and try our luck!"

CHAPTER NINETEEN

BARNEY GETS THE JOB

BARNEY GOT the job. Mr. Marvel appeared to think he could try, at any rate. It seemed a wonderful job to Barney.

"I shall get you new clothes instead of those rags," said Mr. Marvel. "I will pay your lodgings for you. You will have three pounds a week—to start with. A good assistant is worth more than that to me, if he does what he is told!"

"Yes, sir," said Barney, hardly believing his ears. He'd be rich! He could save a bit of money! Miranda should have a new skirt!

"But you understand, of course, Barnabas, that I am a magician, a conjurer, don't you?" said Mr. Marvel. "You understand that my secrets are *my* secrets, and if I have to let you into any of them, you must never say a word to anyone about them. Not even to those three friends of yours."

"I wouldn't dream of it," Barney assured him.

"And about your father," went on the conjurer. "I think I can find him for you. In fact, I am certain I can. I shall cause inquiries to be made immediately and let you know where he is. He may no longer be an actor, of course."

"Yes, sir. I know that," said Barney. "Oh, sir—I'd do anything in the world for you if only you'd find out about my father—and make him believe I'm his son."

"I think I can do that all right," said Mr. Marvel. "I know many strings I can pull. Now, be a good boy to me in every way—and probably by the end of the season you won't want a job any more—because your father will want you instead!"

Barney walked unsteadily to the beach. He could hardly believe his good luck. What a job! And what a reward! He sat down and told everyone about the interview.

"Well, I must say that Mr. Marvel is going to do a lot for you," said Miss Pepper. "He must be a kindly fellow, although he looks so solemn and mournful. Well, it's time you had a bit of luck, Barney!"

That was a very happy morning. The sun shone, the water was calm and warm, and everyone was in high

D

spirits. Loony disappeared, as usual, and all the children wondered what friend he would produce this time.

To their enormous surprise he brought back Mr. Tubby —the gloomy, lugubrious Mr. Tubby. How he had managed to persuade him to join the family circle nobody could think.

Mr. Tubby, however, drew the line at monkeys. Children he would put up with, and a courteous, polite dog like Loony, who deferred to him in every way—but not monkeys. Certainly not monkeys. He stared mournfully at Miranda, who stared back, surprised at such a big dog. She suddenly dipped her hand into a bag of peanuts Barney had bought for her, and threw a pawful at the surprised and annoyed Mr. Tubby.

He gave a deep, enormous "WOOOOF" that startled every one for some distance around. He cast a look of scorn at Loony, turned his back on them all, and lumbered back to the inn.

"There! Now he knows what awful friends you've got, he'll never speak to you again, Loony," said Diana with a squeal of laughter. "Oh dear—how marvellous of Miranda to throw those peanuts straight into his miserable face!"

Barney gave in his notice, and got his week's money. He didn't buy himself clothes as he had planned. If Mr. Marvel was going to buy those, he'd buy something else. So he bought a fine handkerchief trimmed with cobwebby lace for Miss Pepper, a book for Diana, a propelling pencil for each of the boys and a ball for Loony. That was so like Barney!

He went to his new job with delight. It would be easy after the one he had just had, which was a dirty one, as well as hard and heavy. And there would be the thrill of seeing how Mr. Marvel set about finding his father!

Mr. Marvel bought Barney some excellent clothes, and Barney appeared at the inn looking very well dressed for the first time in his life. He grinned shyly.

"Do I look queer? I feel queer! Look at my tie. First time I've ever had one!"

He was full of Mr. Marvel. "He's a funny chap—his bark's worse than his bite. But my word, he's generous! He's already written to somebody who might know my father."

98

Every one's opinion of the conjurer had gone up sky-high. The children told Miss Twitt and the Professor all about how Barney had got his new job. Miss Twitt prattled away, as pleased as they were. But the Professor merely grunted.

"Well, if anyone wants to work with a conjurer I suppose he can! Dangerous job. Mark my words, young man, it's a *dangerous* job!"

He glanced sharply at Barney as he spoke. Barney smiled politely. "Oh, there's nothing out of the way about conjurers, sir. I've been at circuses with sword-swallowers, fire-eaters and the like—they are all quite nice fellows, really."

The Professor gave one of his best snorts. He leaned back in his chair and shut his eyes. The chat was at an end!

Barney began work with the conjurer. He found it quite pleasant. He had to brush and sponge Mr. Marvel's very considerable wardrobe, and to do that, he had to go to his room in the inn. He had to do his shopping for him, and clean all his many pairs of shoes. Mr. Marvel was always complaining that Dummy didn't do them properly.

The conjurer frightened poor Dummy by shouting at him and calling him names that Dummy didn't understand. "Dunderhead! Nitwit! Fumblehands!" No wonder Dummy wouldn't clean his shoes properly for him!

Mr. Marvel initiated Barney into the mystery of his art. He told him what he wanted done on the platform, what cues Barney had to follow and so on. Barney was quick in the uptake and understood everything very easily. He was deft with his hands too, and soon felt that he could do some of the tricks himself that Mr. Marvel did.

"He's a better-class conjurer than you usually find in little shows like ours," he said to the children. "He could get a job in London easily. But he prefers the seaside in summer."

"Has he heard anything about your father yet?" Diana asked eagerly.

"There hasn't been time," said Barney. "But he wrote two more letters yesterday to old friends of his. It would be much easier if I knew my father's name, of course!"

A few days went by, happy and peaceful—and then a rumour flew through the little seaside town. "The police are here! Scotland Yard, they say. It's about that submarine that blew up. It *is* sabotage—someone got to know too much, passed it on—and the result was the blowing up of the submarine!"

The three policemen, all in plain, sober clothes, actually stayed at the inn! This was a terrific excitement. Everyone knew they were the police, of course, and Snubby spent ages staring at them. Had they found out anything? Did they suspect anyone in Rubadub? It was said they had visited the little fair. Had any of the men there something to do with the sabotage?

"Barney always said they were dishonest men," said Roger. "It might be one of them that the police are after."

Mrs. Glump placed a special room at the disposal of the solemn detectives. As Snubby passed the door once, he saw the Professor coming out. He didn't see Snubby, and went slowly up the stairs with bent head. Snubby watched him.

"I bet they've been questioning him! I bet they suspect him! And I bet they're right too! Wasn't he up on the roof that night, watching the blaze? Ought I to tell them?"

On second thoughts he decided not to. After all, he hadn't actually *seen* the Professor—he had only seen the glow of a cigarette, and noticed the Professor's light switched on in his room later on. Regretfully Snubby decided he had better not barge in. But he would keep his eyes open!

Dummy vanished completely when the police arrived. He was absolutely frightened out of his wits. As soon as he knew the three men were detectives he went to earth like a rabbit.

Nobody could find him. Mrs. Glump was cross and worried. "He did that before when a policeman in uniform arrived one day to ask about a lost dog," she said. "Why he's so scared of them I don't know. Oh dear—just when we've got three extra guests in the house too."

Barney offered to help, if Mr. Marvel would let him. Mr. Marvel agreed at once, and went to the police to offer Barney's services if they wanted a good honest lad to clean their shoes and do any other jobs for them. Mrs. Glump, too, was only too glad to accept the offer.

"Thank you," said one of the detectives. "Right. If you can spare him we can make good use of him. We hear he was down at the fair. We'd like to ask him a few questions about the men who employed him."

But except that he knew they were dishonest, Barney could give the police very little information about the men.

"What about the men who go there?" asked one man. "Did you see any getting in touch with your employers?"

"Yes, sir. But I never heard what was said," said Barney. He gave quite a good description of one or two sailors who had visited the place two or three times and spoken to his employers.

"You're employed by a Mr. Marvel now, I believe," said the man. "Getting on all right with him?"

"Yes, sir. He's very good to me," said Barney. "It's a nice job."

"Right. You can go," said the man, and Barney went. He had a room high up in the attics now—he was actually living in the inn with the children, though he had his meals with the staff, of course. It all seemed very wonderful to Barney. Things were going well. And soon Mr. Marvel might hear news of his father. That would be the best thing of all!

CHAPTER TWENTY

NEXT MORNING

"MISS TWITT'S all of a twitter this morning," announced Snubby, the next day. "The police have interviewed her. She's terribly excited about it. She says they asked her all kinds of questions."

"I bet they didn't get anything sensible out of her, then," said Roger. "I wish they'd interview *us*. Not that we've much to tell them. They've talked to Barney. I don't see why *we* should be left out."

"It was only because Barney worked down at the fair," said Snubby. "He thinks the police imagine he might have overheard some queer talk. I say—I do wonder where old Dummy's gone. I miss him."

"I expect he's streaked off at top speed, and is at the

other end of the country by now!" said Roger. "Barney says most circus folk try to keep clear of the police. For all we know, Dummy may have thought they were after him for something."

"He's left all his things behind, the waiter told me," said Snubby. "Poor old Dummy. I did like him."

Miss Twitt sailed up, jingling as usual. A tremendous perfume of Gardenia came with her. She was, as Snubby had so aptly said, "all of a twitter!"

"Pooh!" said Snubby, under his breath, as he got the Gardenia full strength. He removed himself from the room at once, with Loony gasping at his heels. Snubby held his breath till he got outside the door, and then blew out vigorously. Miss Pepper, who was coming in, looked at him in amazement.

"What's the matter, Snubby? Don't you feel well?"

"A bit knocked out, that's all," said Snubby, leaning against the wall, fanning himself with his hands. "Miss Twitt's in there—with a new smell!"

"Oh, don't be so idiotic, Snubby," said Miss Pepper. "I do wish she wouldn't use so many perfumes, I must say—but there's no need to make such a song and dance about it!"

"Good idea!" said Snubby, and produced his imaginary banjo. He began to strum, making his twanging noise, and did a ridiculous step dance in time all round the hall. Miss Pepper began to laugh.

"You're a born comic," she said. "Oh dear, I don't feel as if I want to hear about Miss Twitt's interview with the police all over again. I've had a few words with them myself."

"Gosh! Have you really?" said Snubby, forgetting his banjo. "I say—why are they interviewing everyone here? Do they think anyone has got anything to do with the sabotage?"

"I don't really know," said Miss Pepper. "They've apparently go *some* clue they're working on. I think they're trying to find out how information and orders are passed out and into the Submarine Base. It's practically sealed off from the outside world, you know. Everyone is searched and checked before he goes out. But it can't be anyone *here*—nobody here has anything to do with the Submarine Base."

"I bet I know who it is," said Snubby mysteriously, his mind flashing back to the night of the explosion. "I bet I do!"

"No, you don't, Snubby," said Miss Pepper. "You're just being silly. Oh—good morning, Mr. Marvel. Have you been interviewed too? Snubby here thinks he knows more than the police!"

"And what do you know, young man?" asked Mr. Marvel, with his peculiar smile, that never reached his eyes. "Which of us is the saboteur?"

"What's *that*?" asked Snubby. "Oh—the fellow who did the damage? Aha! That's *my* secret!"

He sauntered off, strumming his banjo again. He wasn't going to tell either Miss Pepper or Mr. Marvel his suspicions of Professor James. They'd only laugh at him. But wasn't the Professor just the person to be mixed up in Big Secrets? He must know an awful lot about scientific things—and any information passed out he would understand—and he could learn it by heart, probably, and then tear up the message.

But how could any message get to him? Well, that was up to the police to find out. Or perhaps he, Snubby, could do a little snooping and find out something.

"I could creep over the roof and peep in at his window, to see if he's doing anything suspicious," thought Snubby, and a swirl of excitement came over him. "I *say*—that would be a smashing thing to do! I'll tell Roger. He could come with me."

Roger was rather doubtful. He agreed that the Professor was the most suspicious person in the inn. He had already told Snubby how he had seen him in the mirror a night or two ago, wide awake, listening to their conversation, although he was pretending to be asleep.

But all the same, creeping over the roof at night to snoop through his window didn't seem too good. "A bit sneakish," said Roger.

"Rot," said Snubby. "If he's a traitor of some sort he deserves to be spied on. If you're not game to do it, I'll do it with Barney. He sleeps up in the attics, and he could easily snoop about at night."

"You and Barney aren't going to have all the excitement," said Roger jealously. "I'm jolly well joining in."

They spoke to Barney about it. He agreed that it would

be exciting to do some snooping round on their own. He thought the old Professor was up to something too.

"He's not such an old crock as he makes himself out to be," said Barney. "And he's not as deaf as everyone imagines either!"

"We know *that*," said Roger. "Right—we'll keep an eye on him—several eyes, in fact. When shall we do our bit of roof-crawling?"

"Wait till the bobbies are gone," said Barney. "I've no doubt they're doing a bit of snooping round too. I saw one of them coming out of the Professor's room yesterday —I bet he'd been doing a rummage round."

"All right. We'll wait a day or two," said Snubby. "They won't be here very long. I say, how does Miranda put up with staying in your room by herself?"

"She's as good as gold," said Barney. "She knows I'm on a job, and she just tucks herself up on a cushion by the window and waits till I'm free to go to her."

"We can always have her when you're busy, you know," said Roger. "Shall we have her now? We're going down to the beach."

"Right. You take her," said Barney gratefully. "I've got a lot to do. Dummy may have been a bit queer in the head, but he certainly managed to get through a lot of work! I must hurry or I shall never get done in time!"

Miranda was perfectly happy to go with Roger and the others. She knew Barney was busy and couldn't rush round with her on his shoulder all the time. So she played happily on the beach. Diana bought her a tiny spade, and Miranda dug with it valiantly, scattering sand all over Loony as soon as he came near.

Loony was still bringing new friends. He brought a tiny Pekinese that day, with a funny little snub nose.

"Isn't that Peke like Snubby?" said Diana. "Miss Pepper, do look at him—he's got *such* a look of Snubby, same untidy mane, same turned-up nose, same . . ."

Snubby threw a bucket of water over her in rage and she screamed, "Don't, you beast! I've got hot in the sun and that water felt icy-cold!"

"Serves you right," said Snubby, pushing away the snub-nosed Peke. "Keep off. You're not my little brother, even though you think you are, after Di's silly remarks!"

Loony dug up a bone he had buried the day before, and proceeded to lie down and gnaw it. The Peke immediately ran up. Loony growled.

"You be careful, Peke," said Roger. "The only time when Loony feels brave is when he's got a bone to protect!"

The Peke suddenly grabbed the bone from beneath Loony's nose and ran off with it. Loony barked in rage and ran after him. The Peke turned, dropped the bone, and faced Loony, yapping fiercely.

"Look at that!" said Diana admiringly. "What a tiny thing to be so lion-hearted!"

Loony ran at the Peke. But the little dog stood his ground and yapped and snapped. He suddenly ran at Loony, snapping his teeth and snarling.

And Loony put his tail between his legs and fled! The Peke picked up his bone and waddled off with it in triumph. He didn't appear again.

"*Well!* Loony ought to be ashamed of himself!" said Roger, disgusted.

"Oh, many a bigger dog than Loony has been put to flight by a Peke," said Miss Pepper amused. "They aren't afraid of anyone or anything. Poor Loony!"

Loony arrived back after about twenty minutes, looking very much ashamed of himself. He sat down by Snubby and looked at him mournfully .Snubby put his arm round him.

"It's all right, Loony. I still love you though you really are a fathead," said Snubby, pulling Loony's long ears gently. "But don't bring any more strangers here—one dog's quite enough!"

Barney passed them, on his way to do some errands for Mr. Marvel. He had to go to the dressing-room at the concert hall on the pier to arrange Mr. Marvel's stage properties for the next show. He whistled gaily.

Miranda shot up the beach and was on his shoulder in a trice. "I'm going on the pier," shouted Barney. "I'll have a few minutes with you when I come back."

"We'll come with you," called Roger.

"No, don't, I can get on without paying now, but you can't," shouted back Barney. "It'd be a waste of money! See you later."

Barney sounded busy and happy. He had been a success with Mr. Marvel at the show. He had been provided with a small silken cloak with stars and moons on it and a round silken cap, rather like the pierrots wore, but with a brilliant star in front of it. He looked extremely handsome in cloak and cap, a simple black tunic and long hose!

"He's a better assistant than I was," Iris told the three children. "He gets on with Mr. Marvel better too. And I must say that Mr. Marvel is very good to him—much nicer to him than he ever was to me. Maybe Barney is cleverer at helping him with his tricks than I was. He's got some new ones since I helped him."

Barney felt that he had decidedly gone up in the world! A job at the inn near his friends—a job on the stage in fine clothes—other new clothes too—and a very fine wage! Barney was very pleased indeed with life.

CHAPTER TWENTY-ONE

A TRICK—AND A PLAN

TWO OR three days went by, days of brilliant August weather when the sea and sky were both deep blue and only a few cotton-wool clouds strayed overhead like lost sheep.

The children were burnt a deep red-brown, and even Miss Pepper began to turn colour too. They all had enormous appetites, and Mrs. Glump began seriously to wonder if she was making any money out of their stay at all! Snubby's appetite seemed quite insatiable.

"You're eating all day long," said Diana. "Honestly, I don't believe you ever stop. And when you can't find anything to bite and swallow, you take that horrible bit of chewing-gum and work on that!"

"Well, it's a comfort," said Snubby, chewing hard. "Though it hasn't any taste left now, unfortunately."

"You're disgusting," said Diana. She really did think Snubby was dreadful with his chewing-gum. She spoke to Roger about it. "Can't we get it out of his pockets and throw it away?" she asked him. "Couldn't you wait till Snubby's gone down to bathe and then take it?"

"No. He takes it with him in his mouth!" said Roger. "But Diana! I'll tell you what we'll do! Listen!"

He whispered to her. She chuckled. "Oh *yes*—that'll cure him! Go and buy some now."

So Roger sped off the beach while Snubby was bathing, and bought a little packet of plasticine. He opened it and took out a small stick. He broke off a bit and began to mould it and squeeze it to get it soft. When he squeezed it flat it really looked remarkably like Snubby's chewed bit of gum!

He and Diana waited their chance. Then Roger substituted the new bit of plasticene for the old bit of chewing-gum, wrapping it up carefully in the bit of paper Snubby kept for his gum.

"Now we'll see what happens," he said to the delighted Diana.

But unfortunately Snubby did himself so well at meals that day, helped out by an ice-cream or two and some sweets, that he didn't remember his precious bit of chewing-gum. So the bit of plasticene stayed in his pocket, waiting.

After tea that day Barney came to them, his face shining with delight.

"Listen!" he said. "Mr. Marvel's had a letter back from one of his friends. He says he thinks he knows my father."

"*Barney!* Not really!"

"Oh, Barney—how wonderful!"

"Gosh—good old Marvel!"

Miss Pepper smiled at the excited boy. "How does the man who wrote to Mr. Marvel know that it's your father?" she asked.

"Well," said Barney, "he said that for one thing this man he thinks is my father used to be an actor and was very fond of Shakespeare's plays—and for another thing his Christian name is Hugo! And that's my second name, you know. My mother must have given me that name after my father!"

"That's very likely," said Miss Pepper. "What did he say your father's surname was?"

"He said it's Johnson, but he doesn't know if that's the name he chose for acting, or whether it's his real name," said Barney. "Isn't it grand, Miss Pepper!"

"Is he like you to look at?" asked Roger.

"He didn't say," said Barney. "He's trying to find out a bit more. He thinks my father was called up in the last war, so he's asking actor friends of his, who were also called up, if they heard of him anywhere."

"It's jolly exciting, all this," said Snubby. "I do wonder what your father's like. He might not be an actor at all now. He might have stayed in the Army—or gone into the Navy or Air Force. He might be an admiral or a general or anything!"

"He might equally well have fallen on hard times and be playing a barrel-organ in the street," said Barney. "I wouldn't mind—so long as he was my father! To find someone who really belongs to me would be wonderful. I never even had an aunt or uncle on my mother's side, I never even remember a granny. You just can't imagine what it would be like to me to find people who were my own."

Barney thought the world of Mr. Marvel. To think he was taking all that trouble! He would be grateful to the conjurer as long as he lived. Barney shone all his shoes till they reflected everything around. He brushed all the conjurer's clothes till they hadn't a speck on them. He cleaned all his stage properties meticulously and never forgot a thing. Mr. Marvel had never in his life had such a willing and trustworthy assistant!

The police went at last. All three detectives slipped out one morning and were not seen again. They were there at breakfast, and then appeared no more. Mrs. Glump heaved a sigh of relief.

"There's nothing for them to snoop about here," she confided to Miss Pepper. "Down in the town perhaps yes—particularly at that Fair. Such a rough lot do go there—especially sailors. That's where any mischief is planned, I don't doubt."

Roger, Snubby, Diana and Barney met on the promenade that morning to discuss the departure of the detectives. They thought they might begin their snooping now. Snubby had dreamt about roof-crawling till he could hardly stop thinking about it.

"Let's have an ice-cream while we're waiting," he said. But no ice-cream man came in sight.

"Oh well—I'll have a spot of chewing-gum," said

Snubby and put his hand into his pocket. Roger looked at Diana and winked. This was the first time Snubby had done any chewing since they had changed over the gum for plasticene! It had exasperated them considerably that Snubby should have shown no interest in his chewing-gum for the last day or two. Still, they could wait!

He took out the piece of paper and unwrapped it. He slipped the grey bit of plasticene into his mouth without even looking at it. He began to chew.

Diana felt she must begin to talk or she would dissolve into some of her helpless giggles. "Isn't the sea grand to-day," she began. "And look at the little frilly white waves at the edge—just like lace. And . . ."

Snubby looked at her in surprise. "What a lot of babble," he said. "You sound like Miss Twitt. She babbles like that!"

He was chewing hard. Then a peculiar expression came over his face. He chewed more slowly. Diana felt an enormous giggle forming in her middle. Roger began to talk fast now, much to Barney's astonishment.

"We'll have to make some plans. We might be able to do something to-night. I thought the Professor looked rather down in the mouth to-day. Maybe the police . . ."

Snubby wasn't listening. He wore a look of great disgust. His mouth fell half open, and he looked desperate.

"Ugh!" he said, and suddenly spat the plasticene right out of his mouth and on to the beach below.

"Snubby!" said Barney, amazed. "You nearly hit that woman on the beach. Whatever are you thinking of?"

"I'll have to get a drink of water," said Snubby, looking very green. "I'll be back."

Diana's giggle burst out of her and she sank back, holding herself tightly. Roger roared loudly. Barney, who hadn't been told the joke, stared in surprise.

Neither Diana nor Roger could explain what the matter was. "Snubby's face!" gasped Diana. "Oh dear!"

"Come on—tell me the joke," said Barney, beginning to laugh himself at the sight of Diana and Roger. At last they were able to tell him. "But don't say a word, will you, Barney?" begged Diana. "If it cures him of chewing-gum it would be too marvellous for words. *Don't* tell him."

Snubby came back, looking better. He sat down on the

seat again. "What was the matter?" asked Barney, trying a keep a straight face.

"It was my chewing-gum," explained poor Snubby, tickling Miranda under the chin. "I think I must have suddenly turned against it, it was *horrible*. I just *had* to spit it out, I couldn't help it. I'm never going to chew gum again, never. Gosh, it made me feel as sick as a wet hen!"

Diana wanted to giggle again. But it would never do to give the game away after Snubby had made such a wonderful resolution. He was never going to chew gum again! It was too good to be true.

"I got a drink of water," said Snubby. "In fact, I drank the whole of the jugful that was on our table. I couldn't seem to get the taste out of my mouth. Who would have thought I'd turn against chewing-gum like that? Well, I felt so sick at even the *thought* of chewing-gum that I made up my mind I'd go up to my room, get the rest of the packet, and throw it away. So up I went."

"Good for you," said Roger, approving heartily.

"And listen to this," said Snubby, dropping his voice suddenly, and looking round furtively as if he thought the promenade might be full of listeners, "Just listen to this. When I got up to my room, there was old Professor James on our landing! He must have been in somebody's room! He doesn't sleep on that landing. He's no business to be there."

The other three were extremely interested. Another black mark against the Professor! "Did he say anything?" asked Roger.

"I said to him, 'Hallo, Professor, lost your way?'" said Snubby. "He just scowled at me and didn't answer. He went downstairs then."

"He might be have been trying to get up those stairs," said Roger.

"He couldn't. The door's locked and the key is lost—or stolen," said Snubby. "It all looked jolly suspicious, anyway. What about doing our snooping to-night? We might see something interesting if we crawled over the roof and peered into his window—always supposing he hasn't drawn the curtains right across."

"Yes, we will," said Roger. "Not Di, though, I'm not going to have her rolling off the roof!"

"I don't particularly want to come!" said Diana. "I'll

110

keep a look-out for you, if you like. But how are you going to get on the roof if you can't get up that little stairway that leads there?"

"Easy," said Roger. "Our window gives on to part of the roof. We can easily get out there and crawl over to where we can peep into the Professor's window."

They all felt very excited. Snubby gave the surprised Loony a loving thump. "Roof-crawling, Loony!" he said. "But not for you, old chap! It's a shame—but I just feel you'll have to be left out of our trip to-night!"

CHAPTER TWENTY-TWO

ALONG COMES AN ADVENTURE

MISS PEPPER couldn't think why the children seemed so mysterious that night. They gave each other winks and meaning looks, and Snubby kept talking about cats on roofs.

"Why do cats like roofs, Miss Pepper?" he said. "Do they go and warm themselves by the chimneys?"

"Why should they?" said Miss Pepper. "Very few chimneys are warm—only those that have a big fire down below. Don't be silly, Snubby."

Roger gave Snubby a kick to warn him to stop. But he went on. "I once knew a nice warm chimney," he said. "It was a lovely place to sit."

"That'll do, Snubby," said Miss Pepper. "If you've got one of your silly fits on, leave the table."

"But I haven't had any pudding," said Snubby. "All right, I'll stop twittering."

Miss Pepper made an exasperated click. But Miss Twitt was engrossed in cold meat and salad and didn't hear Snubby's silly remark.

Barney had a disappointment for them that evening. He met them after their dinner. "I've got to go to the show now," he said, "but I just came to tell you I won't be able to join you to-night. I've got to take a bag with something urgent in it over to the next town after the show."

"Well, you'll be back before midnight I should hope!" said Roger, surprised.

"No, I shan't," said Barney. "I've got to stay the night at Pearley, at the place I take the bag to. It's some clothes Mr. Marvel wants altering in a hurry—some of his stage clothes. He says the old woman I give the bag to will alter them that same night and give them to me to bring back to-morrow morning. Apparently she is always willing to do that for him. So I shan't be able to join you, unfortunately. I'm catching the last train to Pearley. I'm taking Miranda, though."

"What a nuisance!" said Roger. "Well, we'll roof-crawl without you. You can join us another time. I just don't feel we can put it off after getting so worked up about it."

"Of course not," said Barney. "I must fly. So long!"

The grandfather clock in the dining-room chimed a quarter to eight. "What shall we do this evening?" said Diana. "It's fine. Shall we go for a walk?"

"No. I'm tired," said Snubby. "All that swimming we did, I suppose. And I don't want to make myself any tireder because of to-night. I want to be jolly wide awake!"

"Well, let's read then," said Diana. "I've got a good circus story I want to finish. It's got a monkey in it, like Miranda."

It was decided that Diana need not keep awake or do any looking-out for the two boys. There wouldn't be much chance, they thought, of any one knowing they had crawled out of their bedroom window or of any one trying to stop them.

"Di, get Miss Pepper's alarm clock for us out of her room," said Roger. "We plan to roof-crawl after midnight, and we're sure to fall asleep before then. We'll have to have an alarm to wake us up."

"Well, set it and put the clock under your pillow then, or it will wake up every one on our landing!" said Diana. "I expect Miss Pepper will go to bed just after we do—she's such an early bird—and when I know she's asleep I'll creep in and borrow her clock."

Everything went as planned. They went up to bed at a quarter to nine, and Miss Pepper yawned and said she really thought she would come too. Diana winked at Roger. Good!

She slipped into their room with the alarm clock at just after half-past nine. "Will you believe it, Miss Pepper's asleep already," she whispered. "Here you are. I half wish I was coming now."

"Well, you aren't!" said Roger. "We'll tell you all about it in the morning, if we discover anything interesting."

Roger put the clock under his pillow. The alarm would go off and waken him but nobody else. It awakened him all right, and he sat up in bed, startled. Of course—it was only the alarm going off! He scrabbled under his pillow and switched it off. Then he woke the snoring Snubby.

It was difficult to wake Snubby, so Roger got Loony to do it instead. Loony leapt on to him and licked his face lavishly. Snubby sat up and pushed him off.

"What on earth . . ." he began, and then remembered. He scrambled out of bed.

"Don't make a row now, Snubby," warned Roger. "And

tie Loony to the bed leg or he'll try to jump out of the window after us. He won't howl, will he?"

"Not if I tell him not to," said Snubby, and tied Loony up firmly. Loony whined a little, but then lay down patiently.

The two boys climbed out of their window. There was a moon, but the sky was very cloudy, so the light was fitful. They sat on the roof outside their window and looked round.

Not far off was the Professor's window. It had a light shining in it, but to-night the curtains were drawn more closely together and only a small crack showed.

"Still—it's enough to peep through," whispered Roger. "Come on. Keep to the flat. parts, or you'll roll away. It's easy going here."

They crawled slowly, dragging themselves along cautiously in a sitting position. There was no danger where they were, but still it all *felt* very dangerous and exciting. Snubby's heart began to beat quickly.

Just as they came really near to the Professor's lighted window, his light went out! The room was in darkness. How maddening!

"What shall we do?" whispered Roger. "Wait a few minutes, do you think?"

"Yes. Let's get by that tall chimney there. We'll be out of sight if he comes to the window," whispered back Snubby. So they crawled silently to the big chimney. Unfortunately it was not a warm one. Still the night was not cold, so it didn't matter!

They stood by the chimney, hoping against hope that the light would be switched on again. And then Snubby suddenly clutched Roger so violently that he made him jump almost out of his skin.

"Roger! Look! What's that!"

Roger looked in the direction that Snubby was facing. He stiffened in surprise. Some distance to the right, and higher up than they were, a light was flashing. Flash, flash, flash. Flash, flash.

"Signalling," whispered Snubby. "What window is it that the signals are coming from? I say, Roger—this is queer!"

"Let's get nearer that window," whispered Roger. "This is very important, Snubby. For goodness' sake don't make any noise. Let me go first."

114

Keeping in the shadow of chimneys when they could, they made their way very cautiously indeed towards the window from which the signals came. It certainly seemed very high up. What window could it be? It must be the highest one in the inn!

Roger clutched Snubby by the arm and put his mouth excitedly to his ear. "Snubby! That's not a window! That's the skylight trap-door opening off that little stair-case! Why didn't we think of it before?"

So it was. The boys could now clearly see the trap-door thrown back, as the moon sailed out from behind a cloud.

"Who is it signalling?" said Snubby. "We *must* find out, Roger. Gosh, the police were right. There *is* someone here who's acting jolly suspiciously. Is it Professor James? It's funny his light went out just before we saw the signals. I suppose they *are* signals?"

"Of course," said Roger, watching for the next series of flashes. "Those flashes can be seen quite clearly by any watcher in the Submarine Bay if he is in exactly the right place to receive them. That cleft in the cliff might be *made* for signals to and fro! Maybe that is why it *was* made originally—for smugglers or wreckers to signal news or warnings. Whoever is out in a boat on the very spot that can be seen from that high trap-door window is no doubt receiving important messages!"

"It *must* be the Professor," said Snubby. "How can we find out for certain, Roger? We simply must!"

"Well, we daren't go any nearer than this," said Roger. "We don't want to be seen. It's important that the man shouldn't know we've been watching him. I know—you slip back into our room and hide somewhere on the land-ing. Then you'll see the man come down and spot who he is!"

"Jolly good!" said Snubby. "I'll do that. You stay here and watch."

He crawled away from Roger very carefully and quietly. He was strung up and excited. Why, this was another adventure! All of a sudden, in the very middle of the night, there was a smashing adventure! You just never knew when adventures might come along.

He came to his window and climbed in. He made his way to the door, fell over Loony, who was very pleased to see him again, and made much more noise than he meant to.

"Shut up, Loony!" he whispered, trying to push the excited dog away. "That's my face you're pawing. Be quiet. SHUSH!"

At last Loony quieted down. Snubby opened his door and looked out. The landing was in complete darkness. Not a sound was to be heard. Snubby debated where to hide. He wasn't afraid of being seen, the landing was so dark—but if the man had a torch, he might pick out Snubby in its light if he didn't hide himself well.

He shut his door softly. He tiptoed across the landing to a window hung with long curtains. He crept behind them and drew them carefully round him. He stood and waited, his heart working like a piston.

He waited there for a few minutes, his ears strained for any sound. Nothing happened. No noise came, not even the creak of a bit of furniture in the night.

Then Snubby thought he heard a sound. What was it? It was rather like somebody very cautiously clearing his throat. Surely that fellow hadn't come down the stairs so quietly that Snubby hadn't seen or heard him! He listened again.

There! The tiny noise came again—it was a little sniff this time. Snubby stiffened with fright. Good gracious! There was someone on the landing. He was certain of it. Where? Who could it be?

And then the door enclosing the little staircase opened slowly. A little moonlight came through the skylight at the top of the stairway, enough to show Snubby that someone was creeping out of the door. Then it shut just as softly. Who was it? Snubby hadn't been able to make out—but he was absolutely certain it was old Professor James!

CHAPTER TWENTY-THREE

SNUBBY IS NOT LION-HEARTED

SNUBBY, HIDDEN behind the long curtains, heard the little creak-creak of the boards under the landing mats, as somebody went cautiously by. He longed to make absolutely certain that it was the Professor.

He would follow him and see if he went down to his bedroom on the next landing. So he slid out between the curtains and took a step or two towards the head of the stairs. He had completely forgotten there might be somebody else hidden on the landing!

He heard the creak of a stair some way down. He came

to the head of the stairs and began to go down very cautiously himself.

But one of the stairs creaked so loudly that the man he was following heard it. He was now on the landing below. He took fright.

He ran down the remaining stairs at top speed and landed down in the hall. Snubby ran after him.

And somebody ran after Snubby! That somebody who had been hiding on the top landing, as well as Snubby, was coming down the stairs, close on his heels!

Snubby felt a hand clutch at him. He was suddenly terrified. He tore into the big dining-room, which was dimly lighted now and again by the moon. He must hide!

He heard a noise coming from the hall. Somebody was struggling there—struggling with somebody else, panting, trying to keep as silent as possible.

Snubby heard a gasp as one of the two fighters struck a blow. Then came a groan. He gazed desperately round the big dining-room. Where, oh where could he hide? Whatever was going on was something desperate, and he didn't want to be mixed up in it. Who was the Professor fighting?

He was standing by the grandfather clock. It suddenly made the loud whirring noise that meant it was going to strike.

Snubby almost jumped out of his skin. His hair stood on end—and then, with a wave of relief he realised that it was only the old clock. The old clock—why—the old clock would hide him!

Snubby felt for the clasp that fastened the door of the clock over the great pendulum inside. He opened it and got inside, almost falling in, he was so anxious to hide. The fighters were now in the dining-room, swaying this way and that, and they crashed against a table. Snubby pulled the clock door shut and stood trembling inside. The pendulum tried its hardest to swing to and fro with Snubby pressing against it, but it couldn't. It gave up, and the clock suddenly stopped its loud ticking.

But nobody noticed that, certainly not poor Snubby. He could only hear his heart beating, far more loudly than any grandfather clock!

There was a crash as a chair went over. Both the fighters fell on the floor, judging by the thudding and wriggling that went on. Snubby longed to peep out and see

118

who the two were, but he didn't dare to push the clock door open even a crack. It was not Snubby's night for being lion-hearted!

A dog began to bark. It wasn't Loony. He was too far away to hear any noise. It was Mr. Tubby, shut up in Mrs. Glump's little den, with his enormous basket.

The fighters stopped for a moment. Then there was the sound of scampering feet, a click—and silence. One of the fighters had evidently gone. Which one?

Snubby listened with both his ears. The one who was left tiptoed to the hall. Snubby then heard him going up the stairs—creak; creak-creak.

He was gone. Snubby wondered whether it was all right for him to go and find Roger. He was simply longing for Roger! Snubby was always very brave in the daytime, but at night things were somehow different.

He pushed open the door of the clock. He climbed out. At once the pendulum began to swing again and the clock ticked once more. Tick-tock, tick-tock, slowly and deliberately.

Snubby tiptoed to the door in his turn. He didn't like it a bit. He wished he was safely back in the clock. He stopped, thinking he heard a sound. He had! Oh goodness gracious, who was that now? How many more people were there prowling about to-night?

It was somebody in the hall. The moon shone out at that moment and Snubby shrank back into a deep shadow, waiting there, shivering. If any one was in the hall he could jolly well show himself first!

A pair of curtains draped over a big hall window suddenly moved. Snubby nearly screamed. He stood there in his corner, hardly daring to breathe. Who was coming out of the curtains?

But nobody came out. Instead, something was poked through and a brilliant light suddenly shone on poor Snubby, making him gasp. He was caught in the beam of a powerful torch!

It was too much! He tore up the stairs two at a time, gasping and panting, fearing that the one behind the curtain would chase him. But nobody came after him. When he got safely to his room he sank down beside Loony, trembling and terrified. What an awful night! However many suspicious people were there creeping about the inn?

It seemed suddenly to have become a perfect hot-bed of extraordinary happenings!

Loony licked him and licked him, whining because he didn't understand why Snubby was so scared. Snubby remembered Roger. He would still be out on the roof, wondering why in the world Snubby was such a long time. Snubby, feeling much better now, decided to go and get Roger and tell him of the astounding happenings down in the inn.

He climbed out of the window. The moon suddenly swept out again and he saw Roger standing by a chimney. Was he still watching for the flashing signals? Or was he looking into the Professor's window? He would be back in his room by now, no doubt.

He crawled to Roger. "What an age you've been!" said Roger crossly. "The flashes have stopped long ago and there's been no light in the Professor's room, so there's been absolutely nothing to see. What have you been doing? Did you see who came down the stairs?"

"There's too much to tell you out here," whispered back Snubby. "Come back to our room. But, I say—let's peep into the Professor's room first. I've got a reason."

"Got a torch?" asked Roger. Yes, Snubby had. They could shine it quickly into the room.

"But suppose he's there?" said Roger. "He'll be angry."

"He won't do anything," said Snubby. "He'll be too scared! Come on—it's important."

They crawled to the Professor's room, and switched on the torch through the crack in the curtain. The light fell on the bed. No one was sleeping there. Snubby swept the light of his torch swiftly over the little room. It was quite empty, but the door was shut.

"Whew! He's not back yet! Where did he go to then?" wondered Snubby. "I certainly heard him creaking up the stairs after the fight."

"What fight?" asked Roger, astonished.

"Let's get back to our room and I'll tell you all about it," said Snubby. "Come on."

They were soon in their room, and once again Loony gave them an enormous, over-generous welcome.

"Before I tell you everything I must just see if the door of the staircase leading to the roof is still open," whispered Snubby.

He and Roger crept out to see. They shone their torch on to the door. It was shut. It was also locked. And the key was gone!

"The one who has the key is the man we want to look for!" said Snubby. "He's the light-flasher—must be—because he's the only one with the key. And the lock must be well oiled too, because I never even heard him turn the key in the lock."

They went back to their room—but on the way Snubby paused. "What's that?" he whispered. They both listened. Roger gave a chuckle.

"Only the conjurer having a nice little snore!" he said. "I often hear him at night—don't you?"

"Little does he know all that took place here to-night," said Snubby. "I wish old Barney was here."

Once more they went back into their room and, once more Loony flung himself on them rapturously. He simply couldn't understand what game the two boys were playing, but so long as they kept coming back to him he didn't mind a bit!

They sat on the bed, Loony between them. Snubby began to tell his story—how he had hidden on the landing—and had heard someone sniff, and had known there was someone else hiding there; how he had seen the staircase door open, but hadn't been able to see who came out; how he had tracked the fellow down the stairs, only to find somebody trailing him behind.

"And when a hand clutched me I got the wind up," said Snubby. "I flew into the dark dining-room and got inside the grandfather clock."

"*What!*" said Roger, hardly able to believe this extraordinary tale. "You got into the clock? You didn't Snubby!"

"I did. And the pendulum stopped and the clock didn't tick," said Snubby. "And then the two fellows, whoever they were, began to fight. They rolled round the dining-room, they knocked over tables and chairs, they crashed into the clock, they . . ."

Snubby's imagination was beginning to run away with him. He went on, embroidering his tale as he talked. "They were getting quite desperate, and groaning and grunting, when Mr. Tubby barked. He simply barked the place down. I wonder you didn't hear him."

"Don't be silly. You know I was up on the roof. Go on," said Roger. "I can hardly believe all this. To think I was out of all the excitement! Weren't you scared, Snubby?"

"Pooh, *scared*! What do you take me for?" said Snubby grandly. "It takes a lot more than that to scare *me*. But that isn't all, Roger. When Tubby barked, one of the fellows shot away somewhere—towards the kitchen, I think, because I heard a door click. The other went upstairs. I heard him go. I'm sure it was Professor James, though where he is now beats me. Gone to do a spot more flashing perhaps!"

"Is that the whole story?" asked Roger.

"Not quite. When I got out into the hall, meaning to follow the Professor up the stairs, I heard a sound," said Snubby, thoroughly enjoying himself. "And gosh, there was a *third* person hiding! He suddenly pointed a torch at me from behind those big hall curtains, and got me full in its beam. I just turned and hared up the stairs at top speed. I'd had just about enough."

"I should think so," said Roger. "How very extraordinary! What *can* be going on? We'll have to do something about this, Snubby. My word, *what* goings-on!"

CHAPTER TWENTY-FOUR

A GREAT DEAL OF NEWS

THE TWO boys were so very tired after their late night that they both overslept considerably. Miss Pepper came to wake them just as the breakfast gong went.

"Well, really!" she said. "You'll have to go to bed much earlier if you oversleep like this. That's the breakfast gong, listen!"

They didn't remember the events of the night before as they stared sleepily at Miss Pepper. It wasn't until she had gone out of the room that Snubby sat up and suddenly remembered everything.

"Gosh! Do you remember last night? What are we going to do about it?"

"We'll tell Barney first, when he comes back from Pearley," said Roger. But they didn't see him until almost lunch-time. They debated whether to go to the police or not, as the morning went by and there was still no sign of Barney and Miranda.

Then at last they saw him. He was hurrying along the promenade, Miranda on his shoulder. He waved eagerly to them and then jumped down to the beach. Miss Pepper had gone for a walk, so the four children were alone.

"I say," said Barney, his eyes bright. "I've great news!"

"What?" asked all three.

"My father's been found!" said Barney. "Already! Isn't it marvellous. Look!"

He showed them a letter. Attached to it was a typewritten document, looking very official. Barney pointed to it. "Read it," he said.

"'Hugo Paul Johnson,'" read out Roger. "'Aged 40. Born in Westminster, London. Married Teresa Lorimer. Worked as producer and actor, mainly Shakespearian plays. Called up to the Navy for World War. Remained in the Navy on Secret Service. Present whereabouts secret.'"

The typewritten document was signed by someone in the Services. The three children read it again and again. Well, how wonderful! Barney's father was found at last. Except, of course, that his whereabouts were secret.

"Oh, Barney—I'm *glad* for you!" said Diana, and gave him a sudden hug.

Roger and Snubby were very much moved too. They shook hands solemnly with Barney, feeling that the occasion called for some ceremony to mark it.

"What does the letter say?" asked Diana, "the one this document is pinned to?"

"Nothing much. It's just from one of Mr. Marvel's friends to say he's managed to get the information he asked for, and sends it herewith," said Barney.

"If only we knew where your father *was*!" said Diana. "That's the only thing missing now. Can Mr. Marvel find that out too?"

"He *has* found it out!" said Barney proudly. "And all because of something very extraordinary too—he doesn't mind my telling *you* this, but you must absolutely swear you won't tell any one else."

"We swear," said all three breathlessly.

"Well," said Barney, dropping his voice. "Mr. Marvel is more than he seems. *He's* in the Secret Service too."

There was a dead silence as they all took this in. Barney laughed at their astonished faces.

"I thought that would amaze you," he said. "He is a jolly good conjurer, and uses his gift for that as a cover for his Secret Service work. There's been spying and sabotage going on down here—and he was sent to see if he could trace anything. Extraordinary, isn't it?"

"Gosh, yes!" said everyone.

"And," said Barney, his face glowing even more, *"and* one of the men he's in constant touch with happens to be this very Hugo Paul Johnson—my father! Though he didn't know it! He says he's never seen him, only been in touch with him—and where do you think my father is now?"

"Where?" they all said, hardly able to take all this amazing news in.

"In the Submarine Bay!" said Barney. "Isn't that incredible! To think he's so near and I never knew it!"

"It sounds exactly like a story," said Diana. "Oh, I feel as if I want to hear it all again!"

She did hear it again. Barney repeated it from beginning to end—he couldn't talk about it enough. He was so happy about it, so glad that his father was alive and near him!

"Are you going to see him?" asked Diana.

"Yes," said Barney. "But I don't know how or when yet. Apparently there are some very hush-hush enquiries going on at the moment about this blowing up of the submarine. There are traitors among the men over there, and yet they have been checked and double-checked. My father is helping to track them down, and he hands the information on to Mr. Marvel, who sends it to the proper quarters."

"It's too exciting for words!" said Snubby. "I do hope you'll soon see your father. I bet he's exactly like you! You'll recognise him at once!"

"I hope so," said Barney. "I shan't know for a day or two how it can be arranged for me to meet my father—all the men in the bay are under close supervision since the explosion, and no one is allowed to leave the base on any consideration whatsoever. But Mr. Marvel says that if it's possible he'll arrange a secret meeting *some*how—he'll wangle it if he can. And he will too. He's a marvel, that man—and that's not a joke, it's the truth!"

"Barney, we've got some news too—and I bet it would interest Mr. Marvel," said Roger, remembering the night before and what happened. He began to tell him everything, helped and hindered by Snubby, who kept interrupting and adding various bits.

Barney listened in amazement. Diana had already heard it all, of course. "My word!" said Barney. "That really *is* news! What a pity I was away. I could have joined in it all! I had to take those clothes to the old dame who altered them. I didn't get back till after breakfast and then I had lots of jobs to do. My word—what a tale you have to tell!"

"We thought we ought to go to the police," said Roger. "What do *you* think, Barney?"

"I'll tell you what *I* think," said Barney. "Let me tell it all to Mr. Marvel and see what he suggests. Then, if he thinks you should go to the police, he could go with you. They'd be sure to believe every word you say if Mr. Marvel is with you!"

"Oh yes—that's a bright idea!" said Roger pleased. "Will you tell him, then? Don't forget *any*thing, will you? Even the smallest detail might be important. It's a pity he slept through all the excitement—we heard him snoring away in his room when at last we went back to bed."

"Do you know it's a quarter past one?" said Diana suddenly. "No wonder the beach is so deserted. Oh dear— Mrs. Glump won't be at all pleased with us—late for breakfast and now late for lunch!"

"She'll give us her most glumpish look," said Snubby. "Come on, Loony—eats, boy, eats! Dinner, bone, biscuit!"

"Woof!" said Loony happily, and they ran back to the inn at top speed.

"Barney, come and tell us what Mr. Marvel advises as soon as you know," said Diana, as they parted. "We won't say a word to anyone till you've told Mr. Marvel."

Miss Pepper was thrilled to hear about Barney's father. She spoke to Mr. Marvel about it. The children hadn't told her anything except that Mr. Marvel had traced Barney's father and hoped to arrange a meeting. They hadn't, of course, said anything about Mr. Marvel's secret work.

"What wonderful news for Barney, Mr. Marvel," said Miss Pepper to him after lunch. "It's so good of you to take such an interest in him."

"He's worth it," said Mr. Marvel. "A good, trustworthy boy. There are difficulties in the way of arranging a meeting, but it can be done—it can be done! I shall do my best for Barney you may be sure!"

Barney himself appeared at that moment, eager to talk to Mr. Marvel and tell him what the children had related to him.

"Can I have a word with you, please, sir?" he asked. "It's rather important."

Mr. Marvel got up at once. "Excuse me," he said politely to Miss Pepper, and disappeared into the inn garden with Barney. They were there a very long time. Miss Pepper couldn't understand why the three children hung about so, instead of going down to the beach. At last she got cross and chivvied them all out.

"You won't even have time for a bathe before tea if you hang about much longer!" she scolded. "Whatever is the matter with you all? You *are* a lot of dawdlers!"

Barney joined them in an hour, looking really excited. "Sorry I couldn't come before," he said. He glanced at Miss Pepper, half asleep in her chair. "What about a walk? I could do with one!"

"Yes, do go," said Miss Pepper. "I'm getting tired of Loony digging holes all round me. Stay out to tea if you want to. I haven't brought it with me this afternoon as Mrs. Glump didn't seem very pleased about you all being so late for meals to-day."

"We'll have tea somewhere at a shop," said Snubby. "A lobster tea! And I shall have a *whole* lobster," he added as soon as Miss Pepper was out of hearing.

They went beyond the pier and found a very deserted spot. "Now," said Roger, sitting down comfortably, "what did Mr. Marvel say? Tell us every word!"

"Well, first of all, I must warn you that I can't tell you *every*thing Mr. Marvel has planned, or is planning," said Barney. "It's so very secret. But I'll tell you everything I'm allowed to—and you must absolutely swear and promise not to say a word to anyone till Mr. Marvel says you may."

"We absolutely promise," they all said together. They

sounded so solemn that Loony added a grave deep WOOF too.

"Well," began Barney, "he was *most* interested, of course, in the story you told me of last night. He could kick himself for being asleep! He was horrified when he heard about the signal flashes! He says something or other must be being planned again—another explosion, or a theft of valuable plans, or something."

"Did you tell him we suspected Professor James?" asked Diana.

"Yes. And he says we're right to. The detectives who came down suspected him too, but they can't prove anything against him. They told Mr. Marvel that. They know him well, of course. Mr. Marvel can't quite understand about the fighting. He says one must have been the Professor, of course. He doesn't know who the third person is, but he thinks it may be someone in the pay of the Professor. But do you know who he *does* suspect? You'll never, never guess! Have a try."

CHAPTER TWENTY-FIVE

MORE EXCITING STILL!

"DOES HE suspect Mrs. Glump?" asked Diana after a pause.

"No. Try again. It's someone we know quite well."

"The Funny Man?"

"Oh, no! Try again. And don't suggest Miss Twitt because it isn't her either!"

"Give it up," said Roger. "You tell us."

"*Dummy!*" said Barney. "He says Dummy isn't half as stupid as he seems to be. He's a very, very useful go-between, Mr. Marvel says. He's hand in glove with the Professor."

"I don't believe it," said Snubby, shocked to the bottom of his heart. "I liked Dummy."

"Well, do you remember how he disappeared immediately the police came? That was a guilty conscience, Mr.

Marvel says," said Barney. "He was afraid of being caught."

"I just don't believe it," said Snubby. "I never, never shall believe it. Dummy wasn't like that."

"It shows how much cleverer he was than we thought him to be," said Roger, amazed. "Yes—I believe it. I always thought it was funny that he ran away as soon as the police came."

"Well, I *don't* believe it!" said Snubby, getting into quite a rage about it.

"Don't work yourself up, Snubby," said Barney. "You don't know how dishonest and deceitful people can be, even when they seem quite the opposite. You haven't knocked about the world as I have."

"That isn't the point," said Snubby in one of his obstinate moods. "The point is not that I don't recognise *bad* people when I see them—I grant you I may quite well be taken in by them—the point is that I know a *good* person when I see one. And I know Dummy was good, even though he was queer in the head."

"Well, have it your own way," said Barney. "As he's gone, there's not much point in arguing about him. It's quite certain we'll never see him again! He's probably a hundred miles away by now. I liked him too—but there you are! I was wrong."

"Are we to go to the police?" asked Diana.

"Not yet. Not till Mr. Marvel has collected one last bit of evidence he needs," said Barney. "I have a feeling it's the names of the men who are traitors and saboteurs that he's waiting for now. He says he hopes to get this last piece of evidence soon. Perhaps to-morrow. And *I'm* to be in that! I can't tell you how or why—that's really a terrific secret. I shall be able to tell you all about it afterwards. It's all tied up with how I'm to meet my father for the first time."

Barney was quite breathless after his long speech. Roger and Diana were too thrilled for words. Snubby still looked sulky. He simply couldn't believe that Dummy was bad.

"Let's go and have tea," said Diana, and Snubby at once looked more cheerful. Barney gave him a smack on the back. "Sorry about Dummy," he said. "But these things happen, you know."

Snubby didn't answer, but gave an awkward grin. After

that he was more himself again, and he kept his word and ate a whole lobster for his tea.

"How you can do a thing like that I *don't* know," said Diana. "You'll dream to-night all right. We'll hear you yelling and calling for help! And it'll only be the lobster paying you out for your greediness."

They were all restless and excited for the rest of that day. Miss Pepper stood it until after dinner and then announced that they had better go to the pierrot show again. "I really must get rid of you," she said. "You're so fidgety and restless. Go along with you—I'm sure Barney will like you to see him helping Mr. Marvel, now that he's got used to it."

So off they went to the pierrots. The Professor was there again, too, but not Miss Twitt. They all looked with great scorn at the Professor. Ho! He didn't know that they knew all about his horrible doings! However, he took no notice of them at all, but merely sat slumped down in his chair, only waking up a bit when Mr. Marvel came on to do his conjuring, with a very handsome, finely-dressed Barney as assistant.

Barney certainly was excellent, deft, good at any patter necessary, and first class in the mind-reading. Once more the conjurer identified articles taken from the audience, and once more he guessed the long numbers correctly. There were more numbers to-night—six, instead of three. The audience clapped and clapped again, but Mr. Marvel would guess no more than six.

"It is tiring," he said apologetically to the delighted audience. "Mind-reading and number-guessing are the most difficult things to do!"

That night the boys quite meant to sit up and wait for anything else that might happen. But unfortunately they were so tired with the night before that they didn't wake, even when Loony had a bad dream and began barking in his sleep. "Yip-yip-yip!"

Snubby had terrible dreams. He was set upon by men behind curtains, he was involved in a terrific explosion, people sat hard on his tummy, somebody chased him up thousands of steep steps up which his legs could hardly crawl. Oh dear—that lobster tea!

Nobody heard anything during the night at all, not even Barney, who said he was so excited that he hadn't been

129

able to sleep. Mr. Marvel had had another long talk with him, and had promised that when the morning letters came he might be able to tell him if and when he could arrange with him to meet his father.

Barney saw Mr. Marvel after breakfast. His eyes asked an eager question. Had the letter come? Mr. Marvel nodded. "See me at eleven o'clock, when you can get ten minutes off," said Mr. Marvel. Barney went off whistling, Miranda on his shoulder. Not even a scolding by Mrs. Glump for taking things out of the larder made him down in the dumps.

"I took nothing," he said. "I never do. I'm not that sort. Sorry, Mrs. Glump, but if you think I'd take pie and cakes, when you give me them for nothing, don't keep me! I'll go!"

But Mrs. Glump didn't want to lose such a good worker. She still had no news of Dummy and felt sure he would never come back. So she said no more to the indignant Barney and began to wonder if the bright-eyed young waiter was quite as honest as he seemed.

Barney went off to meet Mr. Marvel at eleven o'clock, when he had a break of ten or fifteen minutes. The conjurer was impatiently waiting for him. He took the boy by the arm and walked with him to a deserted part of the promenade. They sat down in a shelter.

"I've arranged everything, Barney," said Mr. Marvel. "It's all planned out well. By this morning's post I had the letter from one of my men telling me that the names of the saboteurs, the men who blew up the submarine, have all been ascertained. But they're dead secret, of course."

"Yes, sir," said Barney.

"They are being sent from the Submarine Bay to me," said Mr. Marvel. "To-night. They will be delivered by hand. But not here, of course, with so many people like Professor James about. Too dangerous! I am to meet the man who brings the names, away out at sea."

"I see, sir," said Barney, excited.

"I can't row," said Mr. Marvel. "So I want you to row me out, Barney, and row me back. Can you do that?"

"Easily, sir," said Barney.

"And, as your reward, Barney, I will tell you this," said Mr. Marvel. "The man who brings the secret document is—your father!"

Barney couldn't say a word. He could only gaze excitedly at the conjurer. So Mr. Marvel had done what he promised! Arranged everything so that he, Barney, could meet his father face to face! His heart swelled with gratitude.

"Now, not a single word of this to anyone, my boy," said Mr. Marvel. "You understand that it has been difficult for me to arrange for it to be your father who brings the list—I have done it because of you. So on no account must you say a word, not even to your three friends, as I told you before—because I myself would get into serious trouble if my plans leaked out."

"You can trust me, sir," said Barney, looking straight at Mr. Marvel with his brilliant blue eyes, more brilliant than ever now, with excitement and happiness.

"Yes. I think I can," said Mr. Marvel. "Barney, be down on the beach at midnight. It will be moonlight then. I will tell you where to row. I shall be there with a boat which I will go and arrange for now. Good-bye, my boy—and remember—not a word to anyone!"

"Sir—before you go—just one more thing," said Barney. "Will my father know me? Does he know he'll meet me to-night?"

"As soon as he has given you the package safely, you can ask him," said Mr. Marvel. "I think you will find that he knows you, Barney! If he doesn't, then come back to me, and I will put things right. He may have found it all very difficult to believe. After all—he didn't even know that he *had* a son!"

He left Barney and went to speak to a boatman about a boat. Barney sped back to the hotel, afraid that he had taken too long for his break. The children were down on the beach. Nobody was about. Barney began to sing at the top of his voice as he polished up some silver.

Mrs. Glump suddenly appeared, looking extremely "glumpish" as Snubby would say, "Barney! What in the world are you thinking of, making a noise like that!"

Barney couldn't tell her what he was thinking, though he was bursting to tell somebody. He was thinking of that evening—the mysterious trip in the boat—the meeting—the man who was his father! What would they both say? Would his father be pleased with him?

Barney looked at himself in the kitchen mirror. Would

his father have his bright blue eyes and corn-coloured hair? He did hope there would be some likeness between them.

The day dragged along for Barney. It went quickly enough for the others. They bathed and swam as usual. They took a boat round the pier and back. They prawned after tea and caught a magnificent collection of enormous prawns which Snubby said he would ask Mrs. Glump to cook for them.

They didn't see Barney till just before dinner. He grinned happily at them.

"Any news?" asked Roger.

"Yes, plenty. Good news too," said Barney. "But I can't tell you any more. You understand why, I know. Things are going to happen to-night! I'll tell you all about it to-morrow!"

CHAPTER TWENTY-SIX

THE MEETING ON THE ROCKS

BARNEY went to bed at half-past ten that night. At least, he went up to his room—but he didn't even lie down or try to get a little sleep, because he was so excited. This was to be such an important night. He was helping someone in the Secret Service—he was also finding his own father!

Barney walked restlessly up and down the little attic room. Miranda was puzzled. What was the matter with him? She sat on his shoulder while he walked, occasionally nibbling his ear gently, just to let him know she was there.

"What shall I call him?" wondered Barney. "Dad? Father? Pa? And I wonder what he's like. Will he want me to go and live with him? Shall I find I've got aunts and uncles—and perhaps cousins. No—I mustn't hope too much. So long as I just find my father that's enough for me!"

Eleven o'clock. Half-past eleven. Twenty to twelve. Time to go!

The boy crept downstairs cautiously, Miranda still on his shoulder. He couldn't leave her behind, she would hate him going off at night without her.

He made his way quietly down the back stair and into the kitchen. He undid a little garden door and slipped out like a shadow.

Soon he was down on the little private beach belonging to the hotel. He knew the boat would be pulled up there somewhere, waiting. In the house the big grandfather clock chimed the quarter to twelve. Barney was early.

He waited on the beach. The moon came out from behind a cloud and flooded him with silvery light. It was a beautiful night. The tide was rapidly going down. It would be easy to row out to sea.

Then he heard a slight noise behind him. It was Mr. Marvel. "You're there—good boy," said the conjurer's deep voice. "Let's go."

The boat was a roomy one. Mr. Marvel sat on one seat, and Barney sat on another, with an oar in each hand. A heap of tarpaulins lay in the stern of the boat, and coils of rope in the bow.

They were soon on the little waves that swelled up near the shore. Barney rowed strongly out to sea. This was one of the greatest nights of his life, he thought. What a piece of luck that he had met Mr. Marvel!

The moonlight dripped from the oars with the sea-water, as Barney rowed. "Over towards that great ridge of rocks," ordered Mr. Marvel. "Look—that ridge stretching out from the land."

"Why, that's where we rowed out to the other day," said Barney. "We went to see Rubadub Whirlpool. It was a fine sight."

"Ah, good," said Mr. Marvel. "It's just near the whirlpool where I am meeting this man—your father!"

"Oh, well—that's easy then. I know the way perfectly," said Barney, and rowed vigorously. Farther and farther out they went, until they came to the end of the great ridge of high rocks. Now Barney knew he must find the entrance to the channel that led to the pool. He pulled over to the rocks and looked for the narrow, rocky entrance.

"There it is!" said Mr. Marvel. "Swing round a bit more, Barney. That's it. Now we're heading straight for the channel."

Soon they were right in the winding little waterway. It looked quite different now, from when Barney had last seen it, on a brilliant sunny day. It looked bigger, darker, more mysterious. The level of the water was much lower too, because it was now just about low tide. It would soon be on the turn.

Barney pulled right up the channel till he heard the sucking, gurgling sound of the strange whirlpool. Then he looked for the mooring post he knew was there.

"Ah—there it is," he said. "I'll just fling the rope over that post, sir, then we shan't get pulled along to the whirl-pool. Once down there we'd never be seen again!"

The boat came to a standstill, held by its rope. Barney jumped out. "What do I do now, sir?" he asked. "How does my father get here—by boat down the channel too?"

"No. He swims here," said Mr. Marvel.

Barney was amazed. "Swims! But how can he? And why? The bay is completely built round by a stone en-closure, surely? And there are great gates built under water to prevent anything from coming in!"

"Your father is a remarkable man," said Mr. Marvel. "He will swim right under the gates and then strike out for these rocks. He has done it before now. It is the only way that he can bring secret information to us. He is a very brave man."

"But why must he do it all so secretly?" asked Barney. "He might be seen and shot by one of our guards on the stone enclosure."

"Quiet!" said Mr. Marvel. "I can hear someone coming. Now, you know what to do! Meet the man, say the pass-word—'Moonlight Night'—and then take the parcel he gives you. It will be wrapped in waterproof cloth. Give it to me and then go back to talk to your father. I don't want to be present because it will no doubt be a thrilling meet-ing for you both."

Barney nodded. He was feeling tense and excited. He, too, could hear someone coming—climbing over the rocks, panting and exhausted after a long and tiring swim. He waited, his heart thumping painfully.

A man came over the top of the ridge of rocks. Except for bathing trunks, his body was bare and dripping with sea water. It glistened like silver in the moonlight. Barney gazed at him.

He was a big fellow with great square shoulders, and a head of dark, curling hair which was drying already.

"Password," he said sharply, when he saw Barney.

"Moonlight Night," stammered Barney. He couldn't see the man's face because the moon chose to go behind a big cloud at that moment.

The man took a package from the back of his bathing trunks. It was wrapped in waterproof cloth as Mr. Marvel had said. He threw it to Barney.

"Catch," he said. Barney caught it, and then hurried to give it to Mr. Marvel. The conjurer caught it deftly.

Good boy. Now go and talk to your father!" he said. Barney turned, almost trembling with excitement. But the messenger was already climbing back over the rocks again! Barney called to him.

"Wait! Wait! Don't you know who I am?"

The man turned. "Why should I?" he asked.

"I'm your son," cried Barney. "Didn't Mr. Marvel tell you! He said you were my father!"

The man threw back his head and laughed. It was a harsh, mocking laugh. "What's he been stuffing you with?" he said. "You don't want to believe a word he says. I'm not even married."

The moon sailed out for a second and Barney caught a sudden glimpse of the man's face. He recoiled in horror. It was a mean, traitorous face—no, no, surely not his father! Barney stared in horror and dismay. The man laughed again, a contemptuous, amused laugh, and then turned to go.

"Just one of his jokes, I reckon!" he called as he went. He disappeared over the top of the rocky cliff, still laughing.

Barney felt suddenly sick. He sat down on a rock. He had left Miranda in the boat—but she suddenly came scampering up to him, chattering in her queer monkey way. She leapt into his arms, and snuggled to him.

"Oh, Miranda," said Barney. "It wasn't him. I can't make it out, I'm all muddled. I don't understand anything at all. Oh, Miranda!"

Then a sudden flame of anger shot him to his feet. Why had Mr. Marvel deceived him like that? What was the point of it? He would demand an explanation—and if Mr. Marvel couldn't give it, Barney would give away his secrets!

He went back to the mooring post, a furious rage making him tremble. But there was no boat there!

"Where's the boat? Miranda, what's happened? Where's the boat?" cried Barney, feeling as if he were in a nightmare.

He ran along the ledge that led to the exit of the channel between the rocks. If he could catch Mr. Marvel he would fight him, strike him till he cried for mercy, throw him out of the boat if he couldn't explain properly what all this meant!

The boat was rounding the end of the rocks as Barney got there. Barney leapt straight into the water, Miranda still with him, and began to swim towards the boat. He shouted.

"Mr. Marvel! Wait! I've something to ask you. WAIT, I SAY!"

Mr. Marvel went on rowing. Barney was a very strong swimmer, and so full of rage that he swam twice as fast as usual! He reached the boat, and tried to hang on to the edge.

Mr. Marvel hit out at him with an oar, and Barney got a crack on the head. "Keep off!" he shouted. "I've no more use for you, don't you understand that? You were a fool to believe all my pretty tales! You deserve all you got!"

"Mr. Marvel! Wait! I don't understand!" shouted poor Barney, still bewildered.

And then, quite suddenly, he *did* understand. He saw it all! Mr. Marvel had used him for his own purposes. He wasn't in the Secret Service. He was a spy, a traitor, in league with other traitors in the Submarine Bay. He had been afraid when he had found out that Barney and the others knew so much—so he had stuffed up the boy with the silly tale of his father. He had got the secret packet he wanted, and now he was off by himself with it, and would escape easily, because Barney would be left marooned on the Whirlpool Rocks.

"Traitor!" yelled Barney, beside himself with rage. "Spy! Wait till I get you!"

"You can't," called back Mr. Marvel mockingly, rowing away. "I've got what I want, thanks to your kind help— and now I'm off to give it to my headquarters—but *not* the names of those who blew up the submarine! Oh no! I've got the plans of the next secret submarine, not a list of names I already know! And long before anyone sees you on these rocks and rescues you, I shall be hundreds of miles away. You were a very stupid boy, Barney. Oh, VERY stupid!"

Barney could have cried with rage. He saw that he could not catch up the boat now. There was nothing for it but to swim back to the rocky reef with Miranda, and hope and pray that someone would rescue him in a day or two.

But wait—what was happening in the boat? There was a yell from Mr. Marvel, and the boat rocked violently. Whatever could be happening?

CHAPTER TWENTY-SEVEN

MAROONED BESIDE THE WHIRLPOOL

Barney clambered on to some rocks and stood up to see what was going on in the boat. The moon now shone as clear as day, and Barney could see everything.

There were *two* men in the boat, not one! Who was the other? Whoever it was, he had attacked Mr. Marvel and was struggling desperately with him. The two men rocked to and fro in the boat and the boat rocked too, almost overturning. Barney was amazed.

Where had the second man come from? Had he crept into the boat out of the sea? Barney held his breath as the two men struggled together. He could hear their panting clearly. Miranda, wet through crept inside his dripping shirt, frightened.

There was a sudden splash. One of the men had fallen into the water. Was it Mr. Marvel? Oh, let it be Mr. Marvel; Barney strained his eyes to see.

But alas, Mr. Marvel was sitting down, rowing away for dear life. The man in the water was struggling and yelling for help.

"He can't swim!" Barney said suddenly, full of horror. In a trice the boy dived into the water again and was swimming strongly to the struggling man.

He slid his arm under the man's back, and began to life-save him, pulling him towards the rocks. Fortunately the man was now so exhausted that he didn't struggle with Barney or drag him under. The boy took him to a rocky ledge, climbed up and dragged the other man up too.

He looked down at him as he lay there, his eyes shut, his chest heaving up and down as he tried to get his breath. Barney saw who he was.

"Dummy! *DUMMY!* Why, it's you. Well, I'm blessed. This beats me. *DUMMY!* Where did you come from? Good gracious, is this all a mad dream?"

Dummy opened his eyes and saw Barney. He managed a very weak smile. Then he sat up suddenly and looked out over the moonlit sea. Away in the distance was the little black speck that showed where Mr. Marvel and his boat were, on their way to land.

Dummy sent out a string of foreign words after the conjurer, and shook his fist violently. Then he turned and patted Barney's knee.

"You save Dummy," he said. "Good boy, Barney, he save Dummy."

"Dummy—for goodness' sake tell me where you came from so suddenly," said Barney. "I can't understand a thing!"

"Dummy in boat all the time," said Dummy. "Dummy know that man is bad, bad, bad. Dummy know he spy. He flash lights, and then—boom-boom-boom. He makes bad things come, that man."

"Go on," said Barney. "Why didn't you tell any one?"

"Dummy silly, Dummy not brave," said the little fellow. "But Dummy watch and watch. And one day that man see

Dummy watching, and he say, 'Ah—I get police. They take you away, Dummy.' "

"And then one day the police did come and you thought they had come for you and you hid away. Poor Dummy!" said Barney, suddenly seeing light. "Where did you hide?"

"Down in cellars," whispered Dummy, as if he thought somebody might be eavesdropping on the rocks. "And at night Dummy come up—eats pies and cakes in larder. Bad Dummy! And Dummy watch all the time at night. Dummy fight with that man too one night!"

"Gosh! So it was you who followed Mr. Marvel and Snubby the other night—and fought the conjurer!" said Barney. "But who was the third fellow? Goodness, this is a peculiar business—everyone watching everyone else! But I still don't know how you got here like this to-night, Dummy."

"Dummy see that man with boat," said the shivering little fellow. "Dummy hear him tell you things and Dummy afraid for you. So . . ."

"So you slipped under the tarpaulins and waited to see what was going to happen!" said Barney. "You must have given Mr. Marvel a horrible shock when you pounced on him. It's a pity he didn't fall into the sea, and not you. As it is, he's won his little game nicely—got rid of me and all I know—made me a fool—and now he's off with those secret papers, and will escape to do a whole lot more damage. He's too clever, that chap!"

Dummy put his hand into his shirt and drew out something with a sly look. "Papers," he said proudly. "Dummy have them!"

Barney gave a yell. "Dummy! That's the packet the other fellow gave me! How did you get it away from Marvel?"

"He put in bag, and then put bag near Dummy," said Dummy. "So Dummy open bag and take package."

"Oh, Dummy—you're a wonder!" said Barney. "He hasn't got his secret papers after all! And unless he looks in his bag for them he won't even know they're not there! Dummy, I could hug you."

Miranda poked her head out of Barney's wet shirt and chattered a little. Dummy stroked her soft little head. "We stay here long, long time?" he asked Barney.

"Till someone picks us up," said Barney, gloomily.

"Gosh, isn't it cold out here in the wind, for all it's a summer night! Let's get down into that sheltered channel. There's a little cave-like place near the whirlpool we could shelter in. I wish we had a boat! Then we could row to land, and catch that hateful fellow!"

They made their way down to the channel. It was certainly more sheltered there. They walked along the moonlit rocks almost to the whirlpool. "Come and have a look at it in the moonlight," said Barney. "I suppose it will be pretty low now it's low tide."

They went to the whirlpool. Certainly it was very low down in its ring of rocks now, and looked quite different from what it had looked the other afternoon. It sucked and gurgled away a good way below them, lighted brightly by the moonlight.

"Hole down there," said Dummy, pointing. "Big, big hole!"

Barney looked. "Yes—that's the entrance to the tunnel that runs all the way to that blow-hole, Dummy."

But Dummy had no idea of what a blow-hole was. He shook his head. Barney looked below the rock that had a great knob sticking out of it, watching the dark place that must be the entrance to the blow-hole tunnel. He suddenly remembered the old tale that the boatman had related to them.

He stood and stared intently at the hole. The whirlpool's waters were about six inches below the bottom of it. Was that old tale true? Was it really possible to squeeze through the blow-hole tunnel at low tide?

"Dummy, I'm going down to that hole. It leads into a rocky tunnel," said Barney suddenly. "The tunnel leads to land—we might be able to escape that way."

"No," said Dummy, shrinking back. "No."

"Well, listen—there's just a chance I could get back before Mr. Marvel escapes," said Barney. "He might think there's no hurry for him to escape immediately, as I'm marooned here. Dummy, I must take that chance. But you can stay here and I'll try to send out a boat for you to-morrow—if I get through safely."

"Dummy go too," said Dummy. "Barney brave. Dummy poor silly man, but Dummy go with Barney."

"Right," said Barney, only too glad to think he would have company in his dangerous struggle through the rocky tunnel. "We must go now if we're going. The tide is creeping in! Once it gets much above the level of that hole, the water will be pushed and sucked along it to the blow-hole —and that wouldn't be at all pleasant for us!"

Barney leapt down like a cat, and Dummy watched him stand in the entrance of the dark little tunnel. Then he bent his head and disappeared inside.

Dummy then dropped down, lightly but clumsily, almost missing his footing. He shuddered as he just prevented himself from dropping into the angry pool a few inches below. Dummy thought it looked alive and ready to clutch at him.

He went into the tunnel. "Barney!" he called suddenly overcome with fright. "Barney!"

"Here!" cried Barney. "Just in front of you. Follow me. Miranda has hopped down and she's leading the way, bless her! Her monkey eyes can see better than mine in the dark. Feel your way, Dummy—there are all sorts of unexpected knobs and ledges waiting to jab you or trip you up."

Barney sounded more cheerful than he felt. It was a horrid little tunnel, and he had to walk bent almost double. It was wet too, and smelt strongly of something sour and bad. Pooh!

Miranda kept running ahead, then coming back and touching Barney's knee to make sure he was following. She didn't seem a bit scared.

It was difficult work, going along the narrow, low-roofed tunnel. In one place it was so narrow that both Barney and Dummy had to go sideways to get through. Once or twice Barney became panic-stricken. Suppose they got held up somewhere? There wouldn't be time to get back before the tide came in—and they would meet the first big surge of water driven up the tunnel to the blow-hole! That would be horrible—they would surely drown! Or worse still, they might be dragged down by the water that ran back to the whirlpool, and end by being sucked into the pool itself!

Barney shivered with cold and fear as he made his way up the tunnel as fast as he could. It was pitch dark, of course, and he had to feel his way at every step. Miranda, however, had no difficulty at all. She went ahead and then came back, then went ahead again time after time.

"Wait, Dummy!" called Barney suddenly. "The roof's
142

gone down low here. I can't even squeeze under it bent double. We'll have to crawl through it. I hope to goodness it doesn't go for far like this, I shall feel smothered to death!"

The roof went down to within two feet of the floor of the tunnel at this point. Barney wriggled painfully along on his tummy, hoping against hope that the tunnel would get no smaller. Why had he believed that tale of the boatman's? It was only a tale, probably. He began to doubt if he and Miranda and Dummy would ever get out of the dark, damp tunnel.

At last he was through the narrow bit. The roof rose up again. Thank goodness! Barney stood up once more and knocked his head against the roof. Then Dummy gave a shout. "There's water behind me, Barney! It's coming, it's coming!"

CHAPTER TWENTY-EIGHT

A NIGHT OF SURPRISES

WATER! That meant that the tide was coming in rapidly then. Water was being sent up the tunnel already! There was no return that way. They could only push on as quickly as possible, hoping that no great surge would race up the tunnel and overwhelm them.

Barney went on grimly, bruising himself badly as he struggled on as quickly as he could. Then he, too, gave a cry.

"The water again! That's the second time! It reached *my* feet then. Keep close to me, Dummy. We may have to help one another."

The water retreated again. The tide was not yet high enough or strong enough to send a wave all the way along the tunnel to spurt out of the blow-hole. But at any moment a bigger wave than usual might come, and they would be swept off their feet, smothered with the surging water.

"It's wider here," gasped Barney. "We can go more quickly. I'm getting so tired, my legs will hardly move along. Are you there, Dummy?"

"Yes, Dummy here!" came Dummy's scared voice. "Dummy hear water, Barney, water!"

The water ran beyond them that time and then retreated again. Barney stumbled on—and then, oh joy! What was that shining ahead of him? A moonlight opening! The blow-hole itself surely!

Dummy gave a shout of warning. "Big one coming, Barney!" Sure enough it certainly *was* a big wave that time. It almost felled them to the ground, and Dummy bumped right into Barney. Miranda leapt into Barney's arms in fright just in time to escape the swirl of water.

"Up to our knees that time," said Barney grimly. "Come on—just a minute more of this and we're out!" He struggled to the moonlit opening. It was quite round, and so big that he could easily get out. He climbed out thankfully, and pulled himself to a rock above the hole. He must have a rest for a moment, it was no good, he simply must!

There was a loud yell from the cave, and a roar of water. Dummy was caught! This was the first wave powerful enough to rush all the way down the tunnel to the blow-hole itself. It had terrific force.

In terror Barney waited. The water burst out of the blow-hole like a spout from a whale. With it came poor Dummy, yelling in fright. He was thrown up in the air like a ball, and then landed with a thud beside Barney, who was covered in spray.

"Oh, Dummy killed, Dummy drowned!" wept Dummy. "Oh, save poor Dummy."

"You're all right," said Barney. "We're both all right. Just did it nicely. Well, Dummy, I should think you are the first man ever to be thrown out of a blow-hole!"

Dummy went all to pieces. He wept and blubbered and sobbed like a child of three. Barney had to put his arm round him and comfort him. "It's all right now, I tell you. We're going to the inn now. We'll get something to eat and drink, and we'll feel fine!"

"Kind Barney," said poor Dummy, and nestled up to him like a child. Barney gave a weak grin. What a night! After all his great hopes, all he had was poor little Dummy sobbing on his shoulder!

He got up at last. His legs felt wobbly after his long struggle in the tunnel. "Come on, Dummy. Back we go. I'll look after you while you're with me."

Dummy followed him like a dog. Barney knew roughly where he was—at the beginning of the great ridge of rocks, where it jutted out from the land. He had only to make his way a little inland, and he would strike a path that led back to the inn.

The blow-hole was very active now, Giant spouts of water came up continually with a tremendous noise. Barney watched one or two. How weird it was—and how horrible it would have been to be caught in the middle of that tunnel when the blow-hole was in action!

He and Dummy and Miranda made their way landwards. It was not very far. There was a little path made by people who sometimes came to watch the blow-hole, and Barney followed it thankfully.

They came at last to the inn. "Let's go in the side gate," whispered Barney. "Do you know if any door is open, Dummy? Which one did you come from to-night?"

Dummy knew an old forgotten entrance, a low wooden garden door that led into a tiny passage. He opened the door and the two went silently in, with Miranda inside Barney's shirt, trying to sleep after her adventure in the tunnel.

"I wonder what's the best thing to do now," wondered Barney. "Telephone the police, I should think. Oh goodness, what's that!"

They had now made their way to the kitchen, meaning first of all to get themselves something to eat and drink. The moonlight shone in at the window—but standing by the larder was a stout, formidable figure, half in moonlight, half in shadow. There was a click—and the room was flooded with electric light.

"And what's the meaning of this?" said the furious voice of Mrs. Glump. "Raiding my larder again, I suppose? You too, Dummy! Where have you been all this time? I've a good mind to telephone the police! I was watching for my larder thief to-night—I knew I'd get him sooner or later. For shame, Barney! What will your friends say?"

Barney interrupted desperately. "We have got to telephone the police ourselves!" he said. "We want them to arrest Mr. Marvel. He's a spy, a traitor! Mrs. Glump, let me fetch Miss Pepper—she'll tell you I'm not likely to tell you fairy tales!"

"I'd rather fetch someone else," said Mrs. Glump astonished. "If there's anything in what you say, I'll certainly fetch him—or better still, we'll go to him! But mind—if you're lying to me, you'll have the police on your track immediately. Such goings on in my inn! I never did hear the likes!"

"Who is it you want to go to?" asked Barney, puzzled.

"Professor James," said Mrs. Glump, which astonished Barney considerably. Professor James! Why, they had suspected him too! He was probably hand-in-glove with Mr. Marvel, so what was the use of getting *him*?

But Mrs. Glump was not to be argued with. She hustled them both in front of her and pushed them up the stairs, dripping wet as they were. She knocked at Professor James's door.

"Come in," said a low voice, and a light was switched on immediately. To Barney's amazement the Professor was sitting in a chair, fully dressed, in the darkness. Whatever for?

"These two have turned up dripping wet with some tale about Mr. Marvel, sir," said Mrs. Glump. "They wanted to telephone the police. So I thought the best thing to do was to bring them to you, sir—knowing what you've warned me to do."

"But what's the use of telling *him* anything," said Barney. "He may be hand-in-glove with Mr. Marvel for all we know! We've spotted him doing some very funny things anyway. I don't want to tell him what's happened to-night. It's absolutely urgent to find out if Mr. Marvel has come back and to arrest him before he gets a chance to escape."

"What do you know about him?" rapped out the Professor, in such a sharp, imperious voice that Barney got a shock. He looked at him sulkily.

The Professor spoke again, more gently.

"Listen, boy. You can trust me. I'm working for the police. Mrs. Glump can tell you that. I'm here investigating some very queer things, and some very queer people. It's your duty to tell me what you know."

Barney was bewildered. "Mr. Marvel said *he* was on Secret Service work, working with the police too, sir," he blurted out. "He said *you* were one of the people they were watching. But oh, sir—this is very urgent. We've got secret papers here, sir. I don't quite know what they are—plans, I think. They ought to be taken care of quickly."

"Where are they?" demanded the Professor, who suddenly seemed years and years younger, eyes, voice and everything! Barney was astounded at the sudden change in him.

"Here," said Barney and put them on the table beside the Professor. He pounced on them, ripped open the waterproof case and pulled out a folded document. He opened it hurriedly and pored over it. He let out an enormous sigh of relief and leaned back in his chair.

"Thank God!" he said, and it sounded as if he meant it from the bottom of his heart. "Our newest and finest plans! Blue-prints worth a fortune to any enemy. We knew they had been copied—and that the fellow was only waiting to pass them out of the Base. Boy, you don't know what it means to have this document in my possession! But this is all very extraordinary! How on earth did you get hold of them?"

"Sir—it's rather a long story," said Barney. "Couldn't you arrest Mr. Marvel first and get him safely under lock and key?"

"You needn't worry. He was seen when he came in late to-night," said the Professor. "There is a man outside his window, on the roof—and one on the landing outside his door. He's safe enough. We were closing in on him, anyhow. But this is just what we wanted to bring matters to a head. Now—what about your story? Would you like to tell it here, to me—or shall I get the police in just to satisfy you that I'm to be trusted?"

"It's all right, sir. I believe you," said Barney. "But I've been so taken in by Mr. Marvel that—well—I began to feel I couldn't believe anybody! I say, sir—was it you who shone that torch on Snubby the other night after he had come out of the grandfather clock?"

"It was," said the Professor. "I, like Snubby and Roger —and Dummy here—have been doing my little bit of snooping too. So *that's* where Snubby was—in the clock! Bless us all, what a boy! It beat me to think where he had gone to!"

Mrs. Glump noticed that Barney and Dummy had begun to shiver. "Sir," she said, "what about going down to the kitchen and letting me poke up the fire for these two? They're shivering. We can lock the doors on ourselves. These two ought to get dry clothes and something hot inside them."

"Down to the kitchen then," said the Professor obligingly. "I could do with something hot myself, Mrs. Glump. All this prowling about at night is cold work."

They all went down to the kitchen, and Mrs. Glump locked the doors. She gave Dummy and Barney dry blankets to wrap themselves in, while she dried their other clothes beside the fire. She set some milk on the stove to heat, and got some meat-pie from the larder.

"Not so bad, Mrs. Glump," said the Professor, eyeing the pies. "Now—what about a heart-to-heart talk while we put away these? You begin, Barney!"

CHAPTER TWENTY-NINE

IN THE MORNING

IT WAS a strange hour the four of them spent, down in the warm kitchen. Barney told his whole tale, and Dummy occasionally added a few words. He was scared of the Professor.

"It seems to me that you children have been doing quite a bit of investigating yourselves," said Professor James. "All that roof-crawling! Extremely dangerous, I should think. And trying to peer into my window! Well, well—you fancied yourselves as a lot of detectives, I suppose?"

"Not really," said Barney. "I'm sorry we suspected you, sir—but what with one thing and another—you know, not finding you in your room that night—and feeling sure you weren't as deaf as you pretended to be—well, we were right on the wrong track, of course, I see that now! I say, sir—who locked that staircase door and took the key?"

"Marvel, of course," said the Professor. "He used that skylight at the top to signal messages to his friends in the harbour, and when he knew you children were messing about up there, he locked the staircase door! He is a bold and wily fellow, is our Mr. Marvel. His real name by the way, is Paulus, and he really *is* a conjurer—a very good one too."

"Yes, but, sir—he doesn't *really* guess those articles I held up," said Barney. "He taught me various ways of putting the question to him. 'What have I here?' meant something in the jewellery line, for instance, and 'What do I hold in my hand?' meant a watch—and so on. And sometimes, sir, he used to have a pal in the audience who lent something—usually with initials on, so that it seemed marvellous when he guessed them."

"I know all that," said the Professor. "In fact, much of his work in that guessing was only a cover for the giving out of code messages. For instance—those long numbers! They were merely a message in code to a sailor in the audience, who would pass on the code messages to higher quarters on his ship—a traitor there, you see!"

"Yes, sir. I see," said Barney. "But he didn't *guess* those numbers, sir. He told me which cards to hold up each night—they were marked in some way so that I knew—and he knew them too, of course. I thought it was a mean trick to play—but there, he was a conjurer, and tricks are their trade!"

"He worked the message into the number code first," said the Professor. "It took up a lot of his time! May I have another pie, Mrs. Glump? Thank you. Most delicious. Well, my boy, your tale is very interesting, and you must be very tired after your struggle through that blow-hole. You're a brave lad, very brave. I'm sorry about that father business—that false letter describing your father—the false meeting—most disappointing for you. You'll have to try again somehow won't you?"

"No, sir," said Barney. "I'm not trying any more. One disappointment's enough. I don't want to talk about it, please, sir. Anyway—I'm glad that fellow I saw *wasn't* my father!"

"You can't give me any really good description of him, can you?" said the Professor.

"Not really," said Barney. "Just a big strong-looking fellow with a mean face, and I think his hair was curly—oh, and he had a crooked little finger, I noticed. Not that that's much use!"

"It may be, it may be," said the Professor, jotting down a few notes.

"Sir—what will Mr. Marvel do when he opens his bag and finds he's not got the secret package after all?" asked Barney.

"I've no idea. Go off his head, I should think," said the Professor. "However—he's safe enough now, even if he takes it into his head to creep down to hunt in the boat for his lost package! But I've no doubt he's fast asleep, thinking he has everything safe—and that you are well and truly marooned on the cliffs. Nice fellow, Mr. Marvel!"

"Can I tell Diana, Roger and Snubby about all this?" asked Barney.

"Not till to-morrow," said the Professor. "Then we shall have everything nicely finished up, I hope. Go to bed now, boy—what's your name—Barney. You've done well. Pity your father doesn't know it all—he'd have been proud of you."

Barney said good night to the Professor, Mrs. Glump and to Dummy, who was sitting blissfully half asleep in front of the fire. Mrs. Glump had told him she would be very glad to have him back in his old job, and that not another word would be said about hiding away in the cellars—or taking food from the larder at night!

Barney was soon in his attic, fast asleep, tired out with excitement and with struggling through the rocky tunnel. He would dream about that many times in his life!

Next morning Snubby and Roger were awakened by a great commotion outside on the landing. There were shouts and yells, and the noise of a struggle. Then it sounded as if two or three people had rolled down the stairs together.

The two boys leapt out of bed, and, followed by a barking Loony, they ran out on to the landing. They saw a peculiar sight. Mr. Marvel was struggling half-way down the stairs with two burly policemen! One had spent the night in a convenient cupboard, the other had come to relieve him—and had arrived at the very moment that Mr.

151

Marvel, shocked to discover the precious package was not in his bag, was about to hurry downstairs to examine last night's boat.

He was in a great hurry—but the policemen were not. They stopped him and suggested he should go back to his room and rest a little longer. Mr. Marvel had no intention of doing this, of course, and a very interesting struggle had developed on the landing, resulting in all three falling headlong down the stairs together.

Barney, attracted by the noise came running up the stairs to see what was happening. He had been helping Dummy with the before-breakfast jobs. Mr. Marvel suddenly caught sight of him.

It gave him a dreadful shock. What! *Barney* here, large as life, when he ought to be shivering out on the rocks waiting until the next boat trip came to visit the famous whirlpool? He simply couldn't believe his eyes. He sat on the stairs and gaped at Barney.

"Where did you come from?" he said weakly.

"From the kitchen," said Barney promptly. "Lost something, sir?"

Those words, of course, told Mr. Marvel that he had not only lost something but that Barney had got it. He gave up at once and went quietly with the two angry policemen, wearing a most bewildered look.

"What's it all about, Barney?" said Snubby, in openmouthed amazement. "Why have they taken Mr. Marvel? Have they got the Professor as well? Did you row out to the rocks? What about your father?"

"I can't answer all those questions at once," said Barney. "But I've got a whole lot to tell you. See you after breakfast!"

Nobody saw Mr. Marvel again. That plausible, wily, traitorous rogue was dealt with in a way that made it quite impossible for him ever to do any damage to anything or anyone again. Every one in the hotel was horrified when they knew that the conjurer was a traitor and a spy.

Iris Nightingale wept and shivered. "I never liked him. He was deceitful and cruel."

The Funny Man stopped being funny for a whole day, and didn't smile once. He was truly shocked.

Miss Twitt sank back into a chair and said she knew she was going to faint. She had felt in her bones that that man wasn't what he seemed. But as nobody paid the slightest attention to what she felt in her bones, she soon stopped thinking she was going to faint and listened with open mouth to all the news going round.

The three children could hardly believe their ears when Barney told them of his night's adventure. "Crawling through that blow-hole! Ugh, how simply terrifying!" said Diana.

"Smashing! I wish I'd been with you," said Snubby.

"Fibber!" said Diana. "You'd have hated every minute."

"I'm sorry about your father," said Roger. "That was a hateful trick to play on you. Don't give up hope, though, Barney. We'll still go on looking."

"I'm not going to bother any more," said Barney, his face clouding over. "After all that looking forward to seeing him—and to meeting him for the first time—and then for it to be nothing but a trick! No—I've finished with looking for my father. If he wants me, he can look for *me*!"

"But he doesn't know about you!" said Diana.

"Then we'll never know one another," said Barney, and he looked very obstinate. "And listen, you three—I don't want you to mention my father to me any more! Do you promise?"

"No," said Diana. "Don't be silly, Barney. Oh, Barney, don't look like that."

"Well, I mean it," said Barney. "I tell you, I've realised it's just a stupid dream of mine. I've done without a father all these years, and now I've made up my mind I don't want one. I don't want any of you to mention him again. See?"

"All right," said the three reluctantly, seeing that Barney was really serious. What a pity! But after all, it must have been a terrible shock to have that awful, heartless trick played on him by Mr. Marvel.

"What was the fellow like, who gave you the package?" asked Roger.

"I couldn't see very well," said Barney. "I wish I'd noticed more about him—but the moon went behind a cloud just then. I know the Professor thinks I've fallen down a bit there—if I could have described the man properly, he'd have been able to put his finger on one of the main traitors in the camp. All I saw was that he was a biggish man, with possibly curly hair—and a crooked little finger'

Snubby suddenly gave a yell. "A crooked little finger! *I* can give a full description of him then—listen!"

He shut his eyes, visualising the two naval men he had seen in the train coming to Rockypool, where they changed for Rubadub.

"Yes—here he is—a clean-shaven fellow—with a big mole on his right cheek—two teeth overlapping each other in front—hairs growing out of his ears—and a misshapen little finger! There—if the police can find that man in the Submarine Service, he's the traitor who gave you the secret papers last night, Barney!"

CHAPTER THIRTY

WHAT MORE COULD ANYONE WANT

AN ASTONISHED voice spoke behind them. "And how do you know all that, young man?"

They all turned. It was the Professor's voice—but could this be the Professor! This spruce, upright, keen-eyed fellow with brown hair instead of grey and no beard?

He laughed at their astonished faces. "I can be myself now," he said. "Good disguise, wasn't it? I was always afraid that Snubby, in one of his wilder moments, might pull off my beard or wig—but mercifully he didn't! Well, Snubby, what about it? Is that true what you were saying just now—or a little invention on your part? Actually, there *is* a man of that description, but we'd no actual proof of his being mixed up with this business.'

"He was in naval uniform when I saw him, sir, and I noticed everything about him, just as I said," said Snubby. "You find him and pin him down—and tell him Barney saw him last night—you'll have got him all right!"

"I rather think you've hit on the right man," said the Professor. "Excuse me—I'm going to telephone and use your bit of information immediately—mole on right cheek —overlapping teeth . . ."

Out he went, quite a different man from the old Professor they had known so well. What a very extraordinary thing! Why, Miss Twitt might turn out to be a policewoman or something! Surely nobody could *really* be quite as silly as Miss Twitt always seemed!

"I'm going to see Dummy," said Snubby, getting up. "I was the only one of us who didn't believe it when Mr. Marvel said Dummy was bad. I'm going to shake hands with Dummy and tell him he's a fine fellow."

And off went Snubby to find Dummy. He was out in the shed in the back-yard, peeling potatoes, and looking very happy indeed.

"Shake, Dummy," said Snubby, holding out his hand solemnly. "Shake! You're a fine fellow! Loony, put up your paw and salute Dummy! That's right. Now, three barks for Dummy—yap-yap-yap, WOOF!"

Loony obliged at once. Dummy was really very touched. He patted Snubby on the arm.

"You good boy," he said. "Funny boy. Good friend to Barney."

"It's a pity about his father, isn't it," said Snubby. "He says he's given up all idea of trying to find him now. You know he really thought he was going to meet him last night, Dummy, don't you?"

"Meet father?" said Dummy, looking bewildered. "Barney have mother, not father."

"Oh, I forgot. You knew Barney's mother, didn't you?" said Snubby. "What was she like? I say—did she ever tell you anything about Barney's father?"

Dummy frowned, trying to think back so many years. "Dummy think," he said slowly. "Snubby—you play your banjo again, and make me think."

Snubby guessed what Dummy meant. He had known Barney's mother in the years when he, Dummy, had played the banjo. The twang-a-twang-twang noise and the sight of Snubby strumming away would bring back memories of those years.

"Twang-a-twang-twang-twang, twang-a-twang-twang-twang!" went Snubby softly, and Dummy sat, lost in thought.

"She so kind to Dummy," said the little fellow. "She tell Dummy her troubles and she make Dummy tell his. She tell Dummy about Barney's father—just a little bit."

"Did she tell you his name?" asked Snubby quickly, resuming his twang-twang noise at once.

"Oh, his name was Barnabas too," said Dummy, his eyes lighting as he remembered. "Barnabas Frederick Martin—so many times she said it."

"What was he like?" asked Snubby, breathlessly. Have you ever seen him? Twang-a-twang-twang-twang!"

Dummy shook his head. Snubby strummed on violently. "Did you ever hear where he lived? Where his home was? Twang-twang-a-twang-twang, zizz-zizz-zizz!"

He had home, yes—nice home, she said. In Cherrydale," remembered Dummy. "His mother cross because he married circus girl. Unkind to poor Tessie. Made her run far away."

"Now we're getting somewhere!" thought Snubby, exultant. "Who would have thought old Dummy could say so much. I'll know how to make him talk another time—twang-twang-a-twang!"

"Dummy!" called a voice, and Dummy jumped. He was brought back to the present so violently that he looked quite ill for a moment. It was the bright young waiter. "Hi, Dummy—where have you put the dusters? Eaten them or something?"

There was nothing more to be got out of Dummy after that. He put on the worried look that meant he wouldn't be able to answer a single question. But Snubby had found out enough. His first thought was to rush to find Barney and tell him the news.

But no, on second thoughts, he wouldn't. Barney might be still obstinate. He might refuse to listen. Of course, Dummy's story *might* have nothing in it. Perhaps, on the whole, he had better tell Miss Pepper. Grown-ups came in jolly useful at times. They always seemed to know what to do in matters of this kind.

So Snubby was soon pouring it all out to an interested and surprised Miss Pepper. She sat and thought for a minute.

"Cherrydale," she said. "I have a friend living near there. I could telephone her and see if there ever was—or still is—a family of the name of Martin, with a son called Barnabas Frederick. I'll go and do it now. Oh, Snubby, it would be too wonderful if it were true!"

It took half an hour to get through to her friend and

find out that yes, there *was* a family called Martin living at Cherrydale—an old lady and gentleman, and a son called Barnabas, and an unmarried sister of his called Katherine. There was also a married brother with four children.

"Miss Pepper! Barney's not only got a father then. He's got a grandmother and grandfather, aunts and an uncle, and cousins!" said Snubby. *"Miss Pepper!* This is smashing! What do we do next?"

"Leave it to me," said Miss Pepper firmly. "And don't say a single word to Barney about it, for goodness' sake. He couldn't bear a second disappointment."

So Snubby left it to Miss Pepper, and quietly and efficiently she went about the very delicate business of contacting Barney's relations. Four days later she called Diana, Roger and Snubby to her in her room. She shut the door.

"I've news for you," she said. "Barney's father is coming down here to-day. He's longing to see Barney and to know if he really is his son that he never even heard about. Oh, children—I've seen a photograph of the father —and he does look so like Barney!"

"Good old Barney," said Diana, with sudden tears in her eyes. "When's the father coming?"

"This afternoon," said Miss Pepper. "I've arranged for Barney to be on the beach with you. I shall send his father there when he arrives—and you three will simply disappear when you see him—and Loony too, of course. You understand?"

"Of *course*," they all said fervently. Dear Barney. It *must* be his father, it *must*!

All four were on the beach that afternoon. Miranda was playing with her little spade. Loony was waiting for her to put it down so that he could run off with it.

Diana was keeping a watch on the promenade. She suddenly gave Roger a nudge. He looked up.

A man was standing up there, tall and well-built. He had thick, corn-coloured hair, brushed back. His eyes were very wide set, and brilliantly blue. His mouth was wide, and his face was brown. He was a grown-up Barney! He stood there, looking rather nervous. The three children rose up silently behind Barney and went to the promenade. Loony followed, astonished at the sudden move. Barney looked round, also astonished.

The man jumped down to the promenade, and walked down the beach. Barney stood up and faced him, wondering what he wanted. Then he stared incredulously. Why—this man was so like him! Who was he? What did he want!

"Your name is Barnabas, isn't it?" said the man.

"Yes," said Barney.

"So is mine," said the man. "I'm looking for a son I've lost for fifteen years—and I hear you've been looking for me."

"Yes," said Barney again, almost in a whisper. "Are you—are you really my father?"

"Just as much your father as you are my son," said the man, deeply moved as he looked at this fine-looking boy with the brilliant blue eyes so like his own. "And you've got a monkey, I see. How strange!"

"Why strange?" said Barney, fondling Miranda, who had leapt up to his shoulder.

"Because your grandmother has a monkey too!" said his father. "How pleased she will be to have a new grandson, Barney. And your aunts and uncles to have a new nephew. And your cousins to have my boy for a cousin!"

Miranda suddenly leapt on to the man's shoulder with a little chattering cry. She began to nibble his ear.

"Let's go for a walk and talk," said Barney's father, and he took the boy's arm. "You've much to tell me. We've got fifteen years to catch up on! It's a long time!"

They walked off together, Miranda still on the man's shoulder. The other three watched them go from a distance. Diana swallowed hard.

"It's come all right," she said. "Barney's got what he wanted. He won't need us any more."

"He will," said Snubby. "Barney's our friend for ever. Isn't he, Loony?"

"Woof!" said Loony solemnly, gazing after the two walking alone on the sands.

"A holiday—a mystery—an adventure—and a happy ending for dear old Barney!" said Roger. "What more could anyone want?"

"An ice-cream," said Snubby promptly. "Who's coming to buy one?"

says...

'Yo-ho-ho for your next book from the Armada ship! There's a cargo of exciting reading for you—so set sail with another Armada book now.

You'll find more titles listed over the page.'

has a whole shipload of exciting books for you

Armadas are chosen by children all over the world. They're designed to fit your pocket, and your pocket money too. They're colourful, gay, and there are hundreds of titles to choose from. Armada has something for everyone:

Mystery and adventure series to collect, with favourite characters and authors – like Alfred Hitchcock and The Three Investigators. The Hardy Boys. Young detective Nancy Drew. The intrepid Lone Piners. Biggles. The rascally William – and others.

Hair-raising spinechillers – ghost, monster and science fiction stories. Super craft books. Fascinating quiz and puzzle books. Lots of hilarious fun books. Many famous children's stories. Thrilling pony adventures. Popular school stories – and many more exciting titles which will all look wonderful on your bookshelf.

You can build up your own Armada collection – and new Armadas are published every month, so look out for the latest additions to the Captain's cargo.

If you'd like a complete, up-to-date list of Armada books, send a stamped, self-addressed envelope to:

Armada Books,
14 St James's Place,
London SW1A 1PF